W9-AAD-256

SNOWBOARD
CHAMP

The #1 Sports Series for Kids

SNOWBOARD CHAMP

Text by Paul Mantell

Foothills Elementary School

10621 234th Ave. E.
Buckley, WA 98321

LITTLE, BROWN AND COMPANY
New York ❧ Boston

Copyright © 2004 by Matt Christopher Royalties, Inc.

All rights reserved.

Little, Brown and Company

Time Warner Book Group
1271 Avenue of the Americas, New York, NY 10020
Visit our Web site at www.lb-kids.com

www.mattchristopher.com

The characters and events in this book are fictitious. Any similarity to real
persons, living or dead, is coincidental and not intended by the author.

Matt Christopher® is a registered trademark of
Matt Christopher Royalties, Inc.

First Edition

ISBN 0-316-79642-5 (hc) / ISBN 0-316-79643-3 (pb)
LCCN 2004102959

HC 10 9 8 7 6 5 4 3 2 1
PB 10 9 8 7 6 5 4 3 2

Q-FF (hc)
COM-MO (pb)

Printed in the United States of America

SNOWBOARD CHAMP

1

The girl is in trouble. Her red hair streams behind her, blown by the fierce wind. Her arms windmill helplessly as she tries to regain her balance — but it's futile. She is totally out of control, her snowboard rushing faster and faster down the steep, icy slope. She hits a mogul and goes airborne! She's tumbling head over heels! She's headed straight for a big tree! Nothing can save her now.

But wait! What's that flash? That blur, coming straight down the slope at breakneck speed? A strong arm reaches out and grabs her hurtling form, snatching her from danger's grasp! The pair streak down the hillside, the girl cradled in someone's strong arms. Finally, the black-clad mystery man cuts his edge deeply into the snow, sending aloft an arc of ice crystals. With

1

a series of side-slips, he brings them safely to the bottom of the slope.

What amazing skill! What athleticism! What daring! She gazes up at him. "Wh-who are you?" she gasps.

He puts her down on the ground, then unlocks her bindings, freeing her feet from her board. He glances up but does not remove his reflective goggles, or the stylish red and black mask that hides his face. "Just call me . . . Snowboard Champ," he says, then pushes off into the blinding sunlight.

"We're now on our final approach into Dragon Valley airport. Please make sure your seat belts are fastened and your seats are in the upright position for landing."

The voice on the loudspeaker interrupted Matt Harper's daydream, and with a sigh, he opened his eyes to reality. He was no superhero. He was just a thirteen-year-old kid being sent away from home. Sure, he'd be staying with his Uncle Clayton, who was as close to a superhero in real life as Matt could think of. But that didn't change the fact that he had to leave the big city, his old neighborhood, his house, his friends — and most of all, his mom.

His mom. Every time he thought of her he felt a

knot tighten in the center of his chest. He hated her *so much!* Why did she have to go and take that new job with the government — a job where the first thing they do is send you overseas for a whole year to countries where practically nobody speaks any English?

"Can't I come with you?" he'd asked.

She'd shaken her head. "I'll be zipping around from city to city, country to country even."

"What are you doing over there, anyway, that's so important?"

He remembered her patient smile. "Oh, complicated stuff. It would bore you."

"Try me."

"Some other time, honey."

"Why, what are you, a secret agent or something?"

She laughed, but there was something phony about it that deepened his suspicions. "You've got some imagination," she said. "Look, I could put you in a boarding school. . . ."

"No thanks," he'd said.

And of course, he didn't want to stay with his dad and stepmom either, in their tiny house, with his three awful stepsisters. *No way.* So living with Uncle Clayton was the obvious and only choice.

It wasn't such a bad option, after all. Uncle Clayton was his mom's younger brother. He was twenty-seven years old. Whenever Matt had come to visit him in the past, they'd gone snowboarding or mountain biking together. Clay was a master boarder, and last year on Christmas break, he had personally tutored Matt in "the way of the board," as he put it.

Clay always had lots of cool ideas, and he enjoyed a lot of the same things Matt did — like junk food and video games. In fact, Matt's mom was always calling Uncle Clayton "an overgrown teenager."

Well, that was cool with him. But leaving all his friends behind *wasn't* cool. Not for a *whole year*. They'd be into all new stuff by the time he got back, and Matt would feel totally out of it. In fact, he felt out of it already. He didn't belong anywhere at the moment. Not back in Chicago, and not in Dragon Valley. The only place he belonged was right here in this airplane, thousands of feet in the air — suspended in space.

He stared out the window at the ski slopes of Dragon Mountain Resort and tried to focus on the positives. This was an awesome place to spend the winter. It was the day after Christmas, and even from up here, he could see that the slopes were crowded with skiers and snowboarders. Matt smiled. They all looked like little ants. Tomorrow, he hoped to be one of those ants. He was sure it wouldn't be too hard to talk Uncle Clayton into taking him. His uncle was always up for a good time.

Matt closed his eyes and balled his hands up into fists as the plane came in for a landing. This part always made him nervous, although he tried to act calm. Only when they had taxied to a stop at the gate did he relax. But when he reached for his backpack in the overhead rack, he felt a sudden queasiness in his stomach. He wasn't sure if it was the lingering effects of the landing or something else. Something about coming here in the first place. Something about it all being a big mistake.

Uncle Clayton met him at the security gate. "Hey, dude! Whoa, you got even bigger! What's Amy feeding you these days?"

"Same old, same old," Matt responded. "You know, gotta supplement it with the occasional bacon cheeseburger."

"I hear ya," Clay said, throwing an arm around Matt's shoulders. "So, you hungry now?"

"Not in the least," Matt said, his queasiness still bothering him. "Hey, what happened to your hair?"

Clay rubbed a hand over his buzz-cut scalp. "Oh. Yeah, I'd forgotten how long it's been since you've seen me. I kinda got tired of the ponytail, y'know? Gotta go along to get along, right?"

"I guess." Matt wasn't sure what Uncle Clayton meant, but he was too nauseated to argue. "There's one of my bags."

"I got it," Clay said, snagging it from between two vacationers who were blocking access to the carousel. "'Scuse me," he told them. "Pardon my reach."

Soon they'd collected all three of Matt's huge bags. His mom had packed everything he owned, it seemed, as if she never expected to see him again. Matt knew that wasn't true, but it still felt like he was begin abandoned, shipped off and out of the way.

"Come on," Clay told him. "My car's out in the lot."

Matt followed his uncle to his beat-up old pickup truck. They hoisted the bags into the back and got in. "So, this all's been tough on you, huh?" Clay began as they pulled out of the lot.

"Kind of," Matt said. "I'm okay, though. Just a little airsick."

"Okay, windows down," Clay said lightheartedly. "Can't have you hurling in here." He laughed, then fell silent for a moment. "So, are you really okay with spending the year here?"

"Most definitely!" Matt said, a little too cheerfully. "It was my suggestion, remember?"

"'Cause I warned your mom. I'm new at this parenting game. So if I mess up, don't hold it against me, okay?"

Matt had to laugh. He could see that Uncle Clayton was as nervous about this as he was. His mom had been right. This was going to be like having a teenage babysitter, except that your parents didn't come home at the end of the night.

Thinking of his mom, Matt's smile slowly faded. "I guess I'm a little down about it. You know, leaving my friends and all."

"'Course. Goes without saying," Clay said, nodding as he steered them through the airport traffic. "I'll tell you one thing, though. The schools here are supposed to be top-notch."

"That's kind of what I'm afraid of," Matt confessed.

"As in?"

"As in hours and hours of homework."

"Ahh, it'll be the best thing for ya," Clay said, a little too sure of himself.

7

"Was it for *you*?" Matt asked.

He'd touched on a sore spot, and he knew it. He watched as Clay stiffened. "I may've dropped out of high school," he said, "but that was because I was a jerk in those days. I got pulled into all the neighborhood stuff, you know. Fighting . . . partying . . . it was only when I decided to leave all that behind that I put my life together. I haven't gone back to that kind of craziness, and I don't intend to."

"Is that why you cut off all your hair?" Matt asked.

"That's for my work," Clay answered. "I'm a new person, dude. I got my high school diploma and my college degree. And now I've got a career going."

"Yeah?"

"Uh-huh. Didn't your mom tell you?"

"She just said you were doing well, working, you know."

"Uh-huh. I'm doing architecture. It's a big firm, I'm like a junior member of the team, so I've gotta play along. You know, the suit and tie, the short hair, the whole works."

"A suit and tie? You?" Matt said, eyes wide.

"Hey, go easy, okay? Like I said, you go along to get

along. You'd do well to remember that when school starts up again after New Year's."

School — ugh. He wasn't ready for that part yet. Not nearly ready. There were still seven days of vacation left, and he knew just how he wanted to spend them.

"Uncle Clayton," he asked, "do you think we could go snowboarding tomorrow?"

Clay smiled, briefly glancing at his nephew. "I thought you might ask me that," he said. "So I took a sick day. You've gotta brush up on your boarding skills, dude."

"Yes!" Matt said. "Thanks, Uncle Clayton!"

"Can't have you falling and breaking your leg first thing, now, can I?" Clay asked, and Matt could see his eyes twinkling.

Clay's apartment looked the same as it did the year before. It was a large, loftlike space in an old, renovated warehouse downtown. On previous visits, Matt had found it hard to sleep at night because of all the neon lights flashing from tourist hotels and restaurants across the street. This time, he would have to do something about that. Maybe black velvet curtains. Yeah, and he could hang black-light posters and get a strobe.

Such were his thoughts as he went about unpacking

that night. It was a lot of work, setting up the room just the way he wanted it. But no matter how much he fooled around with the furniture, it was still not going to be like his room at home. Not even with all his stuff in it. Not even close.

Unfolding a pair of jeans, he removed the framed picture he'd wrapped up for protection. It was a shot of him and his mom when he was five years old. She was wearing her hair in a ponytail, like she used to in those days before his dad left. After that happened, she seemed to age really fast. She'd let her hair get wild, then cut it short. Lately, there was even some gray in it.

Matt frowned. His dad would probably never go gray, never look old. *Life isn't fair sometimes,* he thought. Yes, his mom had had a hard time since then. But this picture reminded him of when she was still young and happy and beautiful.

He put the portrait on the end table by his pillow, facing him, so he'd wake up looking at it every morning. His mom, smiling, with her arms around him.

No, *of course* he didn't hate her. Not really. But why did she have to go away like this and leave him behind?

2

Matt woke up the next morning and raised the blinds, only to realize that the sun was already high in the sky. He'd overslept! "Hey!" he complained as he ran downstairs, still buckling his belt. "Why didn't you wake me? The day's half over already!"

Clay looked up from his plate of eggs, which he'd nearly finished. "Sleeping Beauty!" he said with a grin. "I figured you needed the rest."

"*Sooo* wrong," Matt said. He went to the stove and scraped some egg out of the frying pan into a clean plate. "I need to go *boarding*, not to sleep."

"Relax, we've got all — hey, Matt, will you slow down? You're gonna choke if you eat like that!"

"I'm done," Matt said, ditching his already empty plate in the sink. "Let's go."

"Sheesh!" Clay said with a laugh. "Slow down, partner. The sun doesn't set till four in the afternoon!"

Matt didn't waste another moment. He threw on his old leather jacket, grabbed his snow goggles and gloves, and hurried out to Clay's truck. Clay had already loaded the boards into the back. Minutes later, they were on the road to the mountain.

Dragon Mountain dominated the valley. With its jagged peak sloping downward for several miles from north to south, it looked like the scaly spine of a dragon, ending in a long, curved tail. The mountain was featured on every postcard sold in every store on the town's main street. Matt had also seen the famous silhouette on snowboards, on ski jackets, and in lots of movies. The beauty of Dragon Mountain was spectacular. In fact, if there really had been a Snowboard Champ like the one in his daydreams, this would have been his home. Some cave high up on the mountain's crest, where he could see everything for miles around and ride to the rescue whenever someone was in trouble. . . .

Bolts of lightning are snaking out of the blackness, crashes of thunder bouncing off the mountains. The vibrations loosen a boulder, and it starts rolling down the hill. Picking up snow and size and speed, it hurtles toward an unsuspecting child innocently snowboard-ing below.

"Billy! Billy, where are you?" The child's parents call in vain from the deck of the lodge, scanning the hillside for their son. "There he is — omigosh, there's an avalanche! It's going to catch up with him."

But wait — what's that streak of red and black dashing out of the cover of the trees? The figure carves a sharp diagonal right in front of little Billy, scoops up the child in its arms, and skirts the edge of the gather-ing snowfall, surfing it like a giant white wave.

At the last instant, the figure in black and red goes airborne, flies over a low rock wall, and lands safely on the other side, safe from the onrushing avalanche!

Little Billy's parents fall into each other's arms with relief. "Thank you, Snowboard Champ!" they sob in gratitude. He hands them their baby, then boards off into the darkness, slicing sharp edges between bolts of lightning until they can see him no more. . . .

"Hey, man, you are really out of it this morning," Clay said, elbowing him. "Earth to Matt! Do you read me?"

"Huh?" Matt said, blinking rapidly. "What?"

"We're here, dude. You wanna board, or you wanna sleep some more?"

Matt grinned, yawned, and hopped out of the truck. He grabbed their boards and boots off the back and waited for Uncle Clay to park. Then they went inside and got in the long line to buy lift tickets.

"Man, this place is crowded!" Matt said.

"Gets worse every year, 'specially Christmas week."

Matt looked. There were dozens — no, *hundreds* — of kids milling around, strapping on their boards or boots, shopping for gear or clothes, waiting to buy tickets or sign up for group lessons. He wondered how many of them were local kids and how many were from out of town. Some of them were his age and might even go to his new school. Maybe they'd wind up being future friends of his, he thought, as he looked them over.

You couldn't tell much about a person at first glance, Matt realized. But he couldn't help speculating about each kid. He couldn't help imagining what it would be like hanging out with them.

"You are *sooo* making that up, Riley Hammett!" said a pretty blond girl with braces, punching the boy next to her playfully.

"It's true," the boy named Riley said, a sly smirk on his face. "I have it on good authority."

"Get out of here, he is not!" said a red-haired girl, giggling hysterically.

"If you had ears like him, wouldn't *you* have them pinned back?" the first girl said, and now all three of them giggled together.

"How do they *do* that anyway?" a second boy, smaller than Riley and with a heavy dose of freckles, chimed in. "Is it plastic surgery?"

"No, you dweeb," Riley replied, twisting his knuckle into the top of the second boy's head. "They do it with a staple gun."

"Ow! Really?" the second boy asked, as the others erupted into gales of laughter.

"Nelson, you are such a space cadet," Riley said, shaking his head pityingly. "Yes, of *course* it's plastic surgery. The kind *you* oughta have on your *whole face*." The girls screamed with laughter at this, but Nelson could only manage a halfhearted smile.

Geez, thought Matt. He'd hate to have those kids talking about *him* like that. Back in his old neighborhood in Chicago, kids were tough, but they usually didn't spend much time gossiping. If they did, they'd get jumped for sure. Kids back home didn't like being disrespected. Besides, in his huge school, kids broke

15

off into groups — groups that sometimes argued and caused each other trouble. So you needed all the friends you could get — and you didn't trash-talk about them behind their backs because you never knew when you might need them to watch *your* back.

Uncle Clayton returned with the lift tickets. "Okay, we're set," he said. "Ready to hit the slopes?"

"Let's go!" Matt replied, happy to get out of the crowded building, away from that obnoxious foursome of kids, and onto the lift.

As they left the ground, Matt leaned forward over the safety bar and breathed in the cold, clean mountain air. It burned his lungs, but he loved it anyway. It left his whole body feeling clean and ready for the future.

At the top of the trail, he and Uncle Clayton got off and prepared for their first descent. It had been a year since Matt had last been snowboarding and, not surprisingly, he was a little nervous. Daydreaming about going down the mountain wasn't the same as actually doing it, and he wasn't sure the skills he'd learned last year were still sharp. Still, when Clay said, "After you," he shoved off just the same.

He took it slow at first, being cautious. Clay didn't

pass him, instead hanging back to see how Matt was doing.

He did fine, considering. He did get rattled a couple of times when faster boarders whizzed by him, startling him. And at one steep stretch of this intermediate slope, he carved too steep an angle, started going too fast, and was out of control for a few seconds. He had to windmill his arms and contort his upper body to keep from doing a serious face-plant.

"Not *too* bad, for starters," Clay commented when they got to the base of the hill. "Let's try it again, and this time, try to relax more. You can't concentrate if you're all tense."

Matt nodded and lowered his snow goggles over his eyes as they got back onto the lift. In the four-person chair ahead of them were the same kids he'd heard talking in the lobby of the lodge — that kid Riley and his freckle-faced friend Nelson, along with the blond girl with the braces and the one with red hair who couldn't stop giggling. Riley sat between the two girls and was obviously the center of their attention.

He was a good-looking kid, Matt guessed, but not enough to explain the adoring looks he was getting from the two girls. Matt figured Riley had something else going. He must have been the coolest kid around or something. He also noticed that all of them were wearing expensive designer ski outfits. Matt thought they looked pretty sharp, but truth be told he preferred his own worn leather jacket and jeans. Keeping up with the latest fashion trends had never been his thing.

"Guess what? Spengler broke his arm," Riley was telling the other kids.

"Word?" Nelson said, his eyes widening. "What'd he do, get it caught in the trash bin looking for food?"

More giggles from the girls and a sly smirk from Riley greeted Nelson's little joke. "I heard his old man broke it when he caught him stealing his stogies," Riley said.

"He asked me to sign his cast," said the redheaded girl.

"So, did you?" the other girl asked her.

"Yeah."

"Eeeuw! Courtney!"

"What?" Courtney asked, raising her voice. "Abby, cut it out!"

"That's almost like, I don't know — *kissing* him!" Abby said. The boys laughed and clapped their hands.

"You guys need to chill!" Courtney said, blushing.

"All I wrote was 'Give me a break, Spengler.' It's not like I signed it, 'Love' or anything."

"Courtney loves Spengler," Nelson crooned. "How romantic."

"Puhleez," Courtney said, lifting the safety bar and hopping off the chair before any of the others.

Matt watched as they all got off. Then he lifted the bar on his and Clay's chair. He wondered who this Spengler kid was and why they all thought he was so horrible.

"Ready?" Clay asked, and Matt strapped his back foot onto his board.

Riley and his friends had already started down the hill and were out of earshot. But Matt could still see them. Riley was in the lead, speeding down the hill with skill and ease. The girls were next, going pretty slowly. And bringing up the rear was Nelson, who was having a hard time just staying vertical.

"Ready," Matt said. But he wasn't really. He wasn't concentrating the way Clay had told him to. It wasn't that he was tense. But he couldn't stop thinking about those four kids and the way they'd acted. He sure hoped they weren't from around here, that he never saw them again after today.

He took another moment to collect his thoughts, then let his back heel down to get himself going. This time around, his ride was better. He could feel himself getting into a rhythm as he picked up speed. He made his turns with less effort, letting the board do most of the work for him. He could tell he was going faster, but at the same time, he felt more under control. His hands and hips anticipated every turn, every bump and mogul, and he glided to a stop at the bottom with a sense of freedom he hadn't felt since — well, since the last time he'd been here.

"Awesome!" Clay shouted as he came up behind him. "Hey, dude, you don't need me riding behind you anymore. Just go for it!"

"How 'bout we go do some jumps later?" Matt suggested.

"Sure thing!" Clay said. "Do you remember any of the stuff I showed you last time?"

"Kind of . . . not really," Matt had to admit. "Well, maybe."

"Okay, we'll start over," Clay said with a laugh. "Once a year on the slopes isn't nearly enough to really get good. But this is gonna be your year, Matt. You'll see. Olympic Village, here you come!"

Just then, Clay's cell phone rang. "Hello?" he said into it, then listened for a minute. "Um, I'm kind of busy right at the moment. Did you look at the plans I sent over?" More listening. "But I'm on a sick day. . . . No, I'm fine, it's just family stuff I'm taking care of. . . . Okay — okay. I'll tell you what. I can be over there in an hour, but I've only got a little while. . . . Okay, see you there."

He hung up and turned to Matt. "Sorry, I've gotta do a quick sales pitch. Can you entertain yourself without me for a couple of hours?"

"Sure," Matt said casually, hiding his disappointment. Clay was a master boarder, especially on the half-pipe and the jumps. Without him, Matt probably wouldn't get to learn anything new today. He certainly wouldn't do any jumps without a little refresher course from Uncle Clayton. Waving goodbye to his uncle, he headed back over toward the lift for another run down the hill.

After three hours, Uncle Clayton still hadn't returned. The time had flown by, with Matt doing several more runs on the same slope. By now, he knew its every contour by heart and was making easy, effortless runs.

His boarding was now almost as fluid as last year, when he'd spent every minute of Christmas vacation learning the basics. He remembered falling thousands of times the first two or three days, and laughed to himself. Yes, he'd improved a lot in that one week. Here he was, on the intermediate slope on his first day back — and already bored with it! He felt like he could go up to the next level, but he knew Uncle Clay wouldn't like him doing that without him there.

He could go try some of the other intermediate slopes — Dragon Mountain Resort had more than a dozen of them — but then how would Uncle Clayton find him when he came back?

Matt looked up the hill from the area outside the main lodge. There was the slope with the jumping ramps. If he did some jumping, he might be able to spot Clay in his bright orange parka when he got back from his business meeting.

Clay had taken him jumping once at the end of last Christmas vacation. It had been scary, but Matt had actually landed on his feet once or twice. It was a rush like no other, and Matt had promised himself to really get good at it next year.

Well, next year was now, and Uncle Clayton or no

Uncle Clayton, Matt was tempted to give it a try *right now.* In fact, that's just what he was going to do.

As soon as he got off the chairlift at the top of the jump area, he wished he hadn't been so impulsive. Why was it that, in a place as big as Dragon Mountain, with more than fifty slopes and hundreds of people on them, he kept running into the same four kids? Actually, there were more of them now. Matt counted seven standing in a group around Riley, who was fooling with one of his bindings.

One of the new kids in the group, a tall, chubby boy, was complaining about how crowded it was today. "I don't know why all these people have to come here and ruin everything," he said. "I mean, can't they go snowboarding someplace else? Does everyone have to come to Dragon Mountain?"

"I've got an idea, Perkins," Riley said, looking up with a half-smile. "Why don't *you* leave town and make some space for the rest of us?"

The other kids laughed, but Perkins ignored him. "Seriously, there must be some other slopes in this part of the country. In fact, I know there are. Why don't they go over to Snowbottom, or Craigsmeur, or wherever?"

"Because those places stink compared to here," Nelson said.

"Really," Abby said, rolling her eyes at Perkins. "Maybe *you* should go check them out, Jeff."

"I will if you come with me," Perkins said in a joking tone.

"Whoo-ooo!" everyone in the group said, looking at Abby to see how she would react.

"Not worth it," Abby said. "I'd rather be stuck in a crowd than alone with you."

"Whoo-ooo!" everyone said again.

"Dissed!" Nelson crowed. "Man, she dissed you bad!"

"Shut up!" Perkins said, shoving Nelson, who fell right onto Riley, knocking him over.

"Get off me, you peanut-head!" Riley shouted, pushing Nelson facedown into the snow and scrambling to his feet. "What is *wrong* with you?"

"He pushed me!" Nelson complained, pointing at Perkins and wiping the snow off his face.

"So? Push him back." And with that, Riley gave Perkins a shove, sending him reeling backward into the snow. "Like that."

The snaps on Perkins's down parka popped open, revealing a black sweatshirt underneath. "DRAGONS" was written on it in red letters, surrounded by a yellow tongue of fire. And below that, in smaller yellow letters, was "Dragon Valley Middle School."

Oh, no, thought Matt. These kids were from here, all right. And although they didn't know it yet, he was about to become their classmate.

One of them.

Matt waited his turn, watching as the others took their jumps. The girls, Perkins, and Nelson all took safe, ordinary, simple jumps — and every one of them except Abby went sprawling on their landings. Then Riley showed them how it was done. He got so much air under him that it seemed like he was sailing through space. At the top of his arc, he twisted his arms and made himself spin around 360 degrees, landing perfectly with his arms raised in triumph to cheers and applause from his friends.

So *that* was his big appeal. Matt realized suddenly that in a town like Dragon Valley, being the best boarder among your friends made you popular. Or at least it helped.

And he *did* want to be popular here, if only to escape being made fun of. He wished to heaven he hadn't come up here on the jump slope, but it was too late now. There was no way down but to jump. And so he concentrated extra-hard. He wanted to make a good first impression in case they happened to be watching. Maybe he wanted it too much, because he couldn't seem to shake the tension that was coursing through him.

People were waiting behind him. He couldn't stand there any longer. He started his descent, then pulled himself up into the jump. But he was early and way out of balance. He twisted his body, trying to right himself in time for the landing, but it was no use. He fell, tumbled down the slope, and barreled right into the group of kids from Dragon Valley Middle!

Someone was underneath him. A sudden, hard shove from below rolled him over and off to the side. Riley rose from the snow, his face red with fury and dripping with ice. "*Get off me!*" he shouted.

"I *am* off you!" Matt shot back before he could stop himself.

"Why don't you watch where you're going!" Riley barked. Stepping toward Matt, he shoved him again, just as Matt was getting up. "Geek."

Matt didn't answer this time. He just sat there in the snow and watched as the whole group of kids boarded away toward the lift. He could see them commenting to each other, laughing and looking back at him as if he were from Mars.

Great start, he told himself. The way he was going, it would be a long, long year in Dragon Valley.

3

Matt's first morning at school brought back memories of kindergarten. That was how nervous he felt, washing up, staring at his face in the bathroom mirror. Was that a zit on his nose? No . . . at least he didn't *think* so. Why did he have to have a cleft in his chin? He hated it, even though his mom always told him it was a good feature.

He got dressed with fashion in mind. Normally he didn't consider that kind of stuff, but he wanted to make a good first impression. So he put on his baggy cargo pants; oversized logo sweatshirt; unlaced, beat-up sneakers; and worn leather jacket. He moussed his hair and made sure his teeth were clean. He stared at his reflection once more, then sighed, turned out the light, and went downstairs to wait for the bus.

He tried to calm his nerves by reminding himself that today was Thursday. School was starting midweek because of the holidays, so he'd only have to endure two days of school before having the whole weekend to go boarding with his uncle.

Getting on the bus, he scanned the seats but didn't see any faces he recognized from that first day on Dragon Mountain. But there was a kid with his arm in a cast sitting way in the back of the bus, surrounded by empty seats. Matt threaded his way down the aisle, not really returning the curious glances he was getting from everyone, and went up to the kid with the cast. "These seats taken?" he asked, deadpan.

The boy with the cast grinned. He had long, greasy-looking dark hair, pimples, and an eyebrow ring and a nose ring, and he was missing one of his teeth — the one that would have been his left fang if he'd been Dracula. "Take your pick," he said, gesturing with his cast toward the empty seats that surrounded him.

Matt looked at the cast. "You're Spengler, right?" he said.

"Right," Spengler said, looking surprised. "How'd you know that?"

"I'm psychic," Matt said, nodding his head like Mr. Cool. "Matt Harper. I'm new in town, staying with my uncle."

"Cool," Spengler said, nodding slowly. "Welcome to the armpit of the universe."

Matt laughed uneasily. "Wh-what do you mean?" he asked. "You're kidding, right?"

Spengler's smile was slightly mysterious. "You tell me. You're psychic, right?"

"Ha-ha. No, I mean, it's beautiful here, and I'm into snowboarding, so . . ."

"Yeah, maybe you'll like it here, then. The boarding is unsurpassed. . . ."

"But . . . ?"

"But what?"

"Then why is it the armpit of the universe?"

"Oh. It's the people that stink, not the place."

"All of them?"

Spengler shrugged and made a face. "Most people are sheep, in my humble opinion. Wherever the sheepdog tells them to go, they go. So if the dog's a good one, everything's cool. If the dog's . . . well, a *dog*, so to speak, then you're in trouble."

Matt pictured Riley Hammett in his mind. He wondered if that was the dog Spengler meant, but he didn't ask him. Not yet.

Spengler was different, Matt thought. Probably that was why the other kids thought he was weird and made fun of him. Dragon Valley might or might not be the armpit of the universe. But either way, it obviously stank to be Spengler.

Suddenly, in spite of the fact that he kind of *liked* this kid and his weirdness, Matt wished he'd sat next to someone else.

"Wanna sign my cast?" Spengler asked.

"What for?"

"Everybody's signing it. You might as well join in. Baaa . . . baaa," he added, making sheep noises. A couple of girls seated ahead of them turned around, then looked away again, giggling.

"No thanks," Matt said.

"You don't have to write anything nasty," Spengler assured him. "Just sign your name. It'll help me remember it."

Matt laughed, took out a pen, and signed his name, right next to SPENGLER YOU DWEEB.

The bus pulled into the school driveway, and everyone started piling out. "Nice to meet you," Matt said.

"Yeah. Later," Spengler said, struggling to put his backpack over his shoulders. Matt knew he should have offered to help, but he didn't want to be seen as the friend of the school outcast right off the bat.

In homeroom, he spotted the first of the group he'd seen at the ski slope — the blond girl named Abby. He smiled at her, but she didn't smile back. Instead, she looked him up and down, then turned away and tapped another girl on the shoulder. She whispered something in her ear, and the second girl looked at Matt and giggled.

Now it was Matt's turn to look away. This second girl was really cute, with dark, wavy hair and green eyes the size of quarters. She probably *already* thought he was a geek. A surge of hatred for Abby and her group coursed through him, and he remembered Spengler's words: "Most people are sheep."

Other kids were giving him curious looks, too. Matt noticed that most of the boys were dressed more preppy than he was. He was going to have to either get all new clothes or give up trying to fit in. He remembered Uncle Clayton's short haircut and what he'd said: "You've got to go along to get along." Could Matt get along in this strange new place, so different from what he'd been used to his whole life?

The homeroom teacher, Mr. Evans, an overweight, bald man of about fifty, walked into the room and clapped his hands for attention. "Everybody listen up," he told the class. "We have a new arrival I want to introduce you to. Matt, would you stand up, please?" Embarrassed, Matt got to his feet. "This is Matt Harper. He's from the big city — Chicago." A murmur rippled through the classroom. Matt could feel everyone looking at him differently, as if he were not just new but somehow menacing.

Were they scared of the big city out here in the boonies? Matt wondered. It was possible most of them had never traveled very far from Dragon Valley — but they couldn't really believe what they saw on TV about big cities, could they?

He could hear Spengler's voice in his head: "Baaa . . . baaa . . ."

The rest of the morning passed in a blur. Spengler was in his Spanish class, but since Matt was assigned a seat on the other side of the room from him, they didn't speak. Still, Matt took a moment to really look Spengler over.

Spengler wasn't good-looking, and Matt knew that many kids would make fun of him just for that. He dressed differently from the others, too, but he took his look further than just clothes. Spengler went to extremes — the nose ring and the eyebrow ring were a bit much for Matt's taste, and the kids here, he could tell, were even less down with it.

Come to think of it, Matt didn't see any kids here with spiky green hair or black gothic makeup or anything like that. It was a small school — there couldn't have been more than a few hundred kids altogether — and Spengler was the only one who seemed so set apart from the others.

In English, Matt sat next to Nelson. Nelson gave him a high-five welcome and spoke to Matt in what he must have thought sounded like genuine inner-city lingo. "Yo, bro, wuzzup?" he asked Matt, bopping his head and grinning knowingly. "You be my dog?"

"Hey," Matt said, but gave no other reaction. He could tell Nelson was making fun of him, showing off for the other kids. But to him, Nelson just looked ridiculous, trying to be something he was most definitely not.

Then again, Matt suddenly realized, wasn't *he* thinking of doing the same thing? Hadn't he thought about trading in his clothes for a new, freshly creased pair of Dockers, a polo shirt, and a V-neck sweater? He blew out a big breath as he sat down at his desk. This was *hard*, this fitting-in business. He wished again, with all his heart, that his mother had turned down that stupid job with the government.

At lunch, he caught his first sight of Riley Hammett. The cafeteria itself was pretty small compared to the one at Matt's old school. Riley sat at a table in the center of the room, in the middle of a large group of kids. When Matt walked by on his way to the food line, every head at the table swiveled to follow his progress. A low murmuring began, and he knew they were talking about him again.

But what were they saying? He was dying to know, even if the answer was something horrible. The worst thing was *not* knowing.

The girl from homeroom with the huge green eyes got in the lunch line behind him. "Um, hi," she said, giving him a tentative smile. "You're Matt, right?"

"Right."

"I'm Melissa. Melissa McCarthney."

"Matt Harper." They shook hands awkwardly.

"You and your family just moved to town?"

"Yeah. Well, not my family. Just me, actually."

"Just you?"

They'd reached the place in line where you ordered. "What's good here?" he asked her.

"Good? *Nothing*." She laughed, and so did he.

"Well, let's put it this way — what's not poisonous?"

"Try the pasta," she said. "It's hard to kill pasta, and it probably won't kill *you*."

He ordered the pasta, and so did she. Weird, getting a choice of things to eat. In the cafeteria back home, you ate what they gave you — and it was real slop, too. Not like here. This at least *looked* like real food, even if everyone still complained about it.

Everyone, everywhere, complained about cafeteria food, he knew. So he didn't take the girl's remark too seriously. She was nice, he thought, to come up and introduce herself. She must have guessed how he felt, being the new kid. He wondered if she was just curious, or if maybe she thought he was cute or something. He hoped so, because he sure thought *she* was.

"So, you're like, living with *who*, exactly?" she asked him.

"My Uncle Clayton. He's really cool."

"Uh-huh." She looked faintly troubled for him. "But, um, your mom and dad . . . ?"

"They're divorced," Matt told her. "My mom's away in Asia for a year, and I didn't want to go. She's on some big government job."

"What kind?"

"I dunno, she didn't exactly explain," Matt said with a shrug.

"Maybe she's a spy," Melissa said, giving him an excited look. "You should've gone with her. You could've been a spy, too."

Matt laughed, although he didn't find it funny. It was just that he'd thought the same thing. Wouldn't that be something — his mom, a real spy?

"What about your dad?"

"Huh?"

"How come you didn't go live with him?"

"I didn't want to, that's all." His tone of voice must have told her not to ask any more questions about it, because she quickly changed the subject.

"So, what do you think of this place?"

"The area, or the school?" he asked her, fishing in his pocket for lunch money.

"Both, I guess."

"I don't know about the school yet," he said. "But the valley is cool. I like snow."

"Yeah, I guess you pretty much have to around here. Did you get much snow back in Chicago?"

"Not enough to go snowboarding. Anyway, there aren't any hills."

"You snowboard?"

"Uh-huh."

"Cool!" she said. "I used to board, but this year, I've been so busy I haven't had time."

He followed her to a table and sat down across from her. There were no other kids near them. He could feel her eyes on him, checking him out. He didn't know what to say, so he concentrated on his pasta.

"Maybe we could go boarding sometime," he heard her say.

He looked up, hoping his face wasn't all red from blushing. "You mean together?"

She shrugged. "If you want to."

"Yeah, that'd be all right," he answered, trying not to sound as pleased as he felt.

"How about Sunday?" she asked.

"Uh, sure! Sunday'd be fine."

"Great." She gave him a look that melted him. "Give me your address, and my mom will drive us."

He wrote it down for her.

"See you then!" she said. "Gotta go now."

He stared after her, trying to wipe the smile off his face. "See you before then," he said under his breath. "Way before."

The giggly redheaded girl from the slopes who'd been sitting with Riley and the others caught up to Matt on the way out of the cafeteria. "Hi," she said. "We haven't met. I'm Courtney."

"Matt Harper." He didn't remind her that they actually had met when he'd barreled into Riley.

"I hear you're from Chicago," she said. "What's it like there?"

"What do you mean?"

"I've never been to a city that big. Is it full of gangs and crime and stuff?"

He laughed. "I don't know. There's some, I guess, but it's cool living there. Lots of stuff to do."

"And did you . . . ?" she asked, giving him a sideways glance.

"I don't get you."

"Did you *do stuff*? You know, *bad* stuff?"

He rolled his eyes and shook his head. "What do I look like?" he asked her. "A criminal or something?"

She frowned. "Well, don't get all touchy. I was just asking. I didn't mean to pry."

"Well," Matt said, "Just for your information, Chicago's great. It's way better than here in every way, except for the fact that you can snowboard here."

He half expected her to be offended, but she seemed not to be. "You snowboard?" she asked. "Cool. Are you any good?"

"I'm all right," he said.

She made a laughing sound but didn't smile. "You should meet Riley Hammett," she said. "He's the best boarder in the whole school."

Matt let out a sigh. "Yeah, I kind of already met him."

She looked surprised. "Oh, so, you guys are friends?"

Matt cleared his throat. "Not exactly." Incredible that she didn't recognize him from the other day — but lucky for him!

"Oh. Too bad."

"Why?" he asked her. "What's the deal with Riley, anyway?"

"Well, let's put it this way," she said. "Riley's a cool friend to have, but you don't want to get on his bad side."

"Oh. I see," he said, adding silently, *Too late.*

4

In gym class, Riley and Matt wound up on the same team for indoor soccer. To Matt's amazement, as they lined up next to each other at the start of play, Riley seemed not to recognize him. First Courtney, now Riley. Hmmm . . .

Maybe my helmet and snow goggles hid my face enough to disguise me, Matt thought. *Or maybe Riley just didn't get that close a look — or maybe he'd forgotten all about it!*

Matt considered himself a pretty fair soccer player, but of course, nobody here knew that, so nobody passed him the ball. Matt contented himself with playing good defense, and after one difficult block, he heard Riley say, "All right! Nice play!"

Good, he thought. He could start fresh and make friends with the kid, and everything would be okay.

Riley came over to him after class and said, "Hey."

"Name's Matt," Matt said.

"Riley," said Riley, shaking his hand. "You're new, huh?"

"Yup."

"Funny, I could swear I've seen you before somewhere."

"I don't think so," Matt lied.

Riley shook his head. "I know I've seen you. Ah, never mind, I'll think of it sooner or later."

Matt swallowed hard.

"I hear you're from Chicago."

"Uh-huh."

"I guess you think you're pretty tough, huh?" He stared hard at Matt.

"I guess so," Matt said. "Depends on what you mean by tough."

"I like the way you blocked that kick. Got the body right in there."

"Oh, that. Yeah, I guess I'm tough, then."

Riley nodded. "Cool. I respect that. You don't mess with me, I don't mess with you, okay?"

Again, Matt was mystified, but he just said, "Okay."

"Good. Then stay away from Melissa."

"Melissa?"

"Melissa McCarthney. Don't act dumb with me."

"What is she, your girlfriend or something?" Matt asked.

"None of your beeswax," said Riley. "Well, nice meeting you. Catch you later."

Matt stared after Riley's retreating figure, feeling like he'd somehow done something wrong even though all he'd done was talk to some girl he didn't even know! He vowed to steer clear of Riley if they crossed paths again that day.

Luckily, they didn't. Still, it was only when he had finally arrived back at home and thrown his leather jacket over the back of one of Uncle Clayton's kitchen chairs that Matt finally felt himself relax. He was pouring a glass of milk when the phone rang.

"Hi, honey, it's me."

"Mom!"

"Matt, how's it going there? Everything okay?"

"Yeah, I guess."

"Uncle Clayton says you're settling in nicely."

"Uh-huh."

"How's school? You started today, didn't you?"

"It's okay."

"Just okay?"

"Mom, I don't know yet. I've only been in class one day."

"Well, do you like your classes? Your teachers?"

"They're fine."

"Made any new friends yet?"

"Yeah, lots and lots of 'em. Mom, cut it out, okay? I just got here!"

"Baby, you know, you've got to make an effort. If you're friendly, people will be friendly back."

"Yes, Mom."

"And don't 'yes' me, Matthew. I'm just trying to be helpful."

Yeah? Then why did you go away? he thought. "Hey, Mom, you never did tell me about your job before you left."

"Oh, well, it's complicated, honey," she said, "and this call's so expensive. I'll write you all about it, okay?"

"Sure . . . Mom, you're not a spy or something, are you?" he asked suddenly.

She laughed — nervously, he thought. "Matthew, whatever would make you ask a thing like that?"

"Well, are you?"

"Don't be silly," she said. "You're letting your imagination run away with you. I told you, I'll write to you about what I'm doing in great detail. For now, you just concentrate on *you*."

Agent Harper walks down the main street of the town, the hood of her jacket pulled up over her head. As she goes, she looks this way and that, her eyes full of tension. Under her arm, she carries a package bound with string. She holds it tightly, as if someone might try to take it away from her. And that must not happen — for inside that package is the prototype for the anti-terror nexus control, vital to the defense of the free world!

A black car pulls around the corner, its tires screeching. Now it's coming up behind her, faster and faster. She runs, but it gains on her. She has only seconds to evade it — there! That alleyway! She cuts into it, running for her life. Then she stops. At the end of the alley, the town gives way to the alpine snowfields. She cannot get anywhere on them without skis — and she has no skis.

The black car screeches to a halt and two men get out, brandishing guns. They run down the alley after her.

She steps onto the snowfield, stumbling forward. They are close now. They point their guns at her.

SWOOSH! She is swept up into someone's arms — someone on a snowboard, in a black and red outfit. "Wh-who are you?" she asks.

"Call me Snowboard Champ, Agent Harper," says her rescuer. "Where can I drop you off?"

He deposits her safely at the edge of the forest path. "Just follow that path to the next town," he tells her. Then he pushes off, back into the white alpine wilderness.

Agent Harper stares after him. "I wonder who he really is," she says to herself.

If she only knew!

5

The phone call from his mom had thrown Matt off stride. Here he was, trying to look ahead, make new friends, get adjusted. Hearing her voice pulled him right back into missing Chicago and his home. Maybe it was the bright neon lights from the street below or maybe it was being homesick, but he didn't sleep well that night.

"Everything okay, dude?" Uncle Clayton asked him over breakfast the next morning.

"Huh? Yeah, why?"

"I don't know . . . you look a little out of it."

"I'm okay," Matt assured him.

"Did you have a good talk with your mom?" he asked, watching Matt closely. "I guess she likes her new job."

"I guess," Matt grunted. He avoided his uncle's gaze.

Clay was silent for a moment, then he drained his

coffee cup and said, "Well, I like my job, too. So I'd best be off." He grabbed some architectural drawings from his drafting table, rolled them up, and stuffed them into cardboard tubes. "Hey, you wanna go boarding Sunday? Do a few jumps, maybe tame the half-pipe?"

"Sure!" Matt said, instantly cheering up. But then he remembered. "Oh, wait, could we maybe go on Saturday? I kind of told this girl in school I'd go with her on Sunday," he said.

Clay shot Matt a grin. "Really?"

"It's nothing," Matt said, feeling the blood rush to his cheeks. "I mean, she just asked me if I wanted to go boarding with her."

"Impressive," Clay said in the same gently teasing manner. "*She* asked *you*?"

"Yeah, but I don't know. There's this other kid. . . ."

"Sounds complicated," Clay said, bundling the tubes under his arm and fishing his car keys out of his pocket. "I want to hear all about it tonight. How about over dinner at Bulko Burger?"

"I'm there!" Matt said, returning Clay's smile. His mom would never in a million years have taken him to Bulko Burger.

On the bus ride to school, he sat near Spengler again. He knew everyone on the bus was pegging him as a loser for making friends with Spengler, but he didn't see any of them rushing to get to know him. In fact, so far only Melissa and Spengler had shown him any kind of friendship.

And what was so awful about Spengler anyway? At least he had a sense of humor. Besides, Matt didn't have the heart to pretend he didn't see him back there, all alone. And after all, Matt wasn't a sheep, was he? He could sit wherever he wanted.

"How's it going?" he asked Spengler.

"Foot in front of foot," Spengler replied. "Getting by."

"I hear you," Matt said.

"How about you? Everyone making nice-nice to the new kid?"

"Not everyone," Matt admitted. "You know how it is."

"Oh, I do." Spengler nodded sadly.

"Hey, I never asked you. How'd you break your arm?"

Spengler snorted. "Snowboarding."

Matt waited for him to tell the story, but Spengler didn't, and then they were at the school.

Well, he'd survived the bus ride, at any rate.

Going snowboarding with Melissa was another thing,

however. He was starting to think it was not such a good idea. Riley had warned him to stay away from her, and Matt had already had one run-in with Riley. He sure wasn't looking for another. He believed Courtney when she said it was not a good idea to get on his bad side.

Maybe Melissa would forget she'd asked him to go. He could pretend he'd forgotten, too. He'd go boarding with Uncle Clayton, and Riley wouldn't bother him.

But Melissa was waiting for him in homeroom. With Abby watching the whole thing from her desk, Melissa came right up to him and said, "Hi, Matt!"

"Oh, hi," he said, giving her a pathetic little wave.

"So I talked with my mom about us boarding on Sunday. Is it okay if we pick you up at ten o'clock?" she asked. Her big green eyes bore right through his brain, burning out whatever brain cells were primed to turn and run.

"Yeah, ten's good," he said. "But, um, could I talk to you for a minute in private?"

"Sure. Why, what's up?" she asked, as he led her toward the back of the classroom and away from Abby.

"What's with you and Riley Hammett?" he asked her point-blank.

"Huh?"

"'Cause if you're going out with him or something, I don't want to get in the way."

"*Going out* with him? *Puh-leez.*" Melissa rolled her eyes and clucked her tongue. "He was my *so-called* boyfriend for two weeks at summer camp, and then I broke up with him. He won't stop bothering me, though."

"You mean he still likes you?"

"I guess," she said with a shrug. "Who knows, who cares? I don't like him that much. He's too mean."

"He is, huh?" Matt said, cringing. *Great. Just great.*

"Don't worry about Riley," she said, patting him on the arm. "I mean, we're just going snowboarding together, for goodness' sake. It's not like we're going *out* or anything."

"Right," Matt said, half relieved and half disappointed.

"And even if we were, what business is it of his? Anyway, I'll bet you could beat him in a fight. You're from the hood, right? Everybody there knows how to fight." She winked, gave his arm a squeeze, and returned to her seat.

Right. Everyone from the hood knows how to fight, he thought. *Everybody but me.*

Dragon Valley Middle being such a small school, news traveled fast. In this case, it traveled like lightning. Everywhere Matt went that day, he could feel kids' eyes on him. He could hear the whispering behind him that stopped whenever he turned around to see who it was.

In the cafeteria, he felt like every eye was on him, but whenever he tried to catch people staring at him, they looked away just in time to avoid being caught at it. Except for Riley. Riley stared right back at him with what could only be described as the evil eye.

Matt thought he knew why, and in gym, Riley confirmed it. "What did I tell you yesterday?" he asked.

"Huh?"

"Don't act stupid with me. You know."

"Oh. About Melissa?"

"Yeah. Your new snowboarding buddy."

"You heard, huh?"

"I couldn't help hearing," Riley said. "Everyone's talking about it."

"Everyone should keep their mouths shut," Matt said, looking around the gym in annoyance at the other kids, who were watching this little spat develop. *Spengler was right*, he thought. *Baaa . . . baaa . . .*

"I'm gonna have to teach you the way things work around here," Riley said. He put an arm around Matt's shoulders, then clamped down tight like an iron claw.

"What do you mean?" Matt asked him, wincing in pain. Riley was at least four inches taller and twenty pounds heavier than he was.

Riley leaned close and whispered into Matt's ear, "You show up at the slopes with Melissa, and you'll find out what I mean."

Matt's shoulder hurt for the rest of the day. When he got out of bed the next morning, he noticed two bruises where Riley's fingers had dug in. Riley had meant to intimidate him. But instead, Matt found he was getting angry. Any thought of canceling the snow-boarding date with Melissa vanished as he stared at the black-and-blue marks.

Still, Matt was glad Melissa had suggested Sunday instead of Saturday. It gave him a day to practice his moves on his snowboard. Lots of kids from school were there, and many of them said hello to him. He returned their greetings and introduced Clay to them but didn't want to hang out with them. He was here with his uncle.

Then he caught sight of Riley, surrounded as usual

by his group of friends. Riley returned his glance, then looked beyond him as if to see who else Matt was with. He must have realized Melissa wasn't there, because he gave Matt a slow smile and nod. It was as if he were saying, "I see that you did what I told you to."

That made Matt even madder, but it also made him a little nervous. How would Riley react tomorrow, when Matt showed up here with Melissa instead of Uncle Clayton?

He pushed the thought away quickly. He'd asked Clay to work on his jumps with him, and his uncle was only too happy to oblige.

"We'll start with some ollies first," Clay said.

They rode the lift to the top of one of the intermediate slopes, one with a lot of small moguls on the way down. "Okay, here's the deal," Clay said. "You get some speed, then move your weight to the back of the board, so the tip is coming up off the snow." He demonstrated on the flat ground, and Matt tried to imitate him. "Then push off your back foot, jump up, and lift the board off the snow. Here, watch me, then you try it."

It was fun for Matt to watch Clay make his way down the hill. Clay was tall and thin, almost like a beanpole, and when he did airborne tricks and jumps, he flew sky-high. He did an ollie first, then pulled up on one side of the slope and shouted back up, "Okay, now you!"

Matt leaned into the hill and started his descent. As he approached the mogul, he crouched slightly at the knees, then pushed off just as he hit the top. He kept his balance in the air but landed a little hard.

"Keep your knees bent until you're back on the ground," Clay advised him, demonstrating on the next mogul as they made their way to the bottom of the hill.

They worked on landings some more, then on getting more and more air in their jumps. "Make sure you do a nice turn after you land," Clay told him. "It'll help control your speed so you don't go flying into someone."

Been there, done that, Matt said to himself. But he kept his mouth shut.

They did half-cabs — 180-degree turns while riding fakie. "Don't worry, these take a lot of practice," Clay counseled when Matt had trouble nailing the jumps. "Keep your body centered and straight. Remember to land flat."

Finally, at the end of the day, Clay taught him to do 360s. "Use your upper body to start the spin," Clay said, demonstrating with a gorgeous jump.

"I don't know if I can do this," Matt shouted down to him.

"Come on, try it!" Clay called back.

Matt did. To his surprise, he nearly landed it. In fact, his surprise was probably the reason he got distracted and wound up falling.

"Never mind, that was a good one till the very end," Clay told him as he picked him up out of the snow. "You keep practicing those. And remember how I told you to fall."

By the time they got home, Matt was sore all over. He ate a quick dinner, then collapsed into bed, wondering how he was going to go boarding again tomorrow. But he knew that he would drag himself to the slopes somehow, for two reasons. One, he wanted to get to know Melissa better. And two, he wanted to show Riley that he wasn't afraid of him.

6

The next day, Melissa's mom drove them both to Dragon Mountain. "Nice to meet you, Matt," she said, looking him over as he got into the car. Everyone was looking him over these days, and it was starting to make Matt feel really uncomfortable.

They said goodbye to Mrs. McCarthney at the resort's gate and walked together to the main lodge to buy their lift tickets. "I'm not that good at boarding," Melissa confessed. "So don't make fun of me, okay?"

"I don't make fun of my friends," Matt told her. "Anyway, I haven't been boarding that many times myself. I only learned last year at Christmas break."

"So you've only gone like, what, seven times?"

He shrugged. "Maybe nine or ten. I don't know. Anyway, I'm not exactly the master. That would be my Uncle Clayton. He's awesome. You should see him do jumps!"

Matt was enjoying himself, happy just to be in the company of someone so nice. But his good time was cut short almost before it got started. No sooner had they gotten their lift tickets than Riley's voice rang out behind them.

"Well, look who's here!" he said with an air of false cheer. "The two lovebirds. Tweet-tweet-tweet!" All the kids around Riley laughed, and Matt could feel his face get hot with the rush of blood.

Melissa stood her ground. "Riley, you're such a jerk," she said. "Come on, Matt. Let's go."

"Hey, Harper!" Riley said, stopping Matt in his tracks. "Not so fast. We've got a score to settle."

"I'm not gonna fight you, Riley," Matt said firmly. "There's nothing to fight about."

"Fight?" Nelson repeated, clueless. "There's gonna be a fight? Cool! What about?"

Matt guessed that it wasn't generally known that Riley still liked Melissa.

"Shut up, Nelson," Riley said, waving him off like an annoying fly. "Nobody's gonna fight anybody. We're just talking about a gentlemanly contest."

"Contest?" Now it was Matt's turn to play echo.

"A snowboarding contest. I hear you're world-class."

59

Matt snorted and shook his head. "Where'd you hear that?" he asked.

Riley ignored the question. "Jumps and tricks, me against you."

Matt disliked the idea intensely. Either he lost the contest and looked like a jerk in front of everyone, or he won and made a jerk out of Riley — which, much as he would enjoy it, he knew would only make things worse. "I don't think so," he said.

He started to protest that he wasn't good enough to engage in contests yet, but he could see there was no point in arguing. Riley was intent upon humiliating him in front of Melissa and all the other kids. He decided that the worst thing of all would be for everyone to think he was a coward. "All right," he finally agreed.

Riley led the way to the jump area. The way the other kids followed him reminded Matt once again of what Spengler had said about sheep and a sheepdog. Watching them made him more determined than ever not to be one of Riley's flock.

"I still don't get what this is all about," Nelson said, as they pushed their boards along the flat area that led to the lifts.

"Harper here is supposed to be a world-class snow-boarder," Riley explained.

Matt frowned. "I still don't get where you heard that."

Riley gave him a sly glance. "Rumor has it" was all he would say.

"Well, who started that rumor?" Matt asked.

Riley shrugged. "I don't know, man. Maybe you." He looked Matt right in the eye.

"Yeah, and maybe not," Matt said with a scowl. This would get him nowhere. The only way to deal with Riley's challenge was to beat him at his own game and deal with the consequences later.

When they got to the top of the hill and hopped off the lift, Riley laid down the terms of his challenge: "How 'bout five jumps each, everybody scores it one to ten, and we just add up the totals?"

"Fine," Matt said. "Whatever you say."

"And no points if you fall." He stared hard at Matt.

Matt stared right back at him. "I won't fall," he said.

When he said it, he believed it. But when he lined up for his first jump, doubts started to creep into his brain. He'd really gone and done it now. He'd left himself totally out on a limb by guaranteeing he wouldn't fall. Only yesterday, practicing with Uncle Clayton, he'd fallen a dozen times! And now, on the day after, he was sore and stiff all over. Why had he opened his mouth like that? What an idiot!

All of a sudden, Matt realized how much smarter it would have been just to walk away from the challenge. But now it was too late, so he tried to get himself ready. He would keep it simple on the first jump, then go from there, building his confidence one step at a time.

"You first," he told Riley.

"What's the matter? You chicken?"

"No. It was your challenge. So you should go first."

"He's right, Riley," Melissa said, crossing her arms in front of her.

Riley gave her a long look. "All right," he finally said. "Who cares? It's all the same to me. This contest is only ending one way, anyhow."

He lined up in front of Matt, waited until the field was clear between him and the ramp, then headed down it, crouching low as he gained speed. Right at the end of the ramp, he lifted off, high into the air, his arms spread out to either side. He landed smoothly, then arced in a half-circle and came to a stop. He looked up and waved, acknowledging the applause from the other kids, who were whooping it up.

"Ten!" Nelson crowed. "It's a ten!"

"I give it a nine," said Abby.

"Nine and a half," Courtney ventured.

The other kids gave Riley similar marks. Even Melissa gave Riley a nine.

Now it was Matt's turn. He tried to do just as Riley had done, keeping his first jump simple and smooth. His nerves, however, were fighting him all the way. He wound up going into his takeoff a second early, costing him height and making him wobble a little on the landing. He got sixes and sevens, and a single eight from Melissa.

On his second jump, Riley decided to get fancy. He did a wiggle-waggle with his legs in the air, back and forth twice, before making another perfect landing.

"Am I supposed to match whatever you do?" Matt shouted down to him.

"Do whatever you want!" Riley shouted back, as he collected another round of nines and tens.

Matt would have liked to do something incredible — a full somersault, or even a double full somersault —

but of course he couldn't do that. He couldn't do anything like that! All he could do, or at least had done once, was a 360 turn, and the chances of him pulling it off now were slim to none. He decided to go with another regular jump, just pulling up his knees to his chest in midflight before landing.

This he was able to do almost perfectly, and to his surprise, he got a nice round of applause from the spectators back at the top of the ramp. His marks were almost as good as Riley's — which seemed to really tick Riley off. He shoved two kids on his way to the starting line. "Watch this!" he muttered under his breath, then shoved off, pointing his body as far forward as he could.

Maybe it was because he'd leaned forward too far, or maybe it was just from trying too hard, but from the moment he went airborne, Riley was off balance. He tried to right himself, but it was too late. He fell on his landing, head over heels, and was lucky to avoid getting hurt.

According to Riley's own rules, that jump got him zero points. Matt started crunching numbers in his head, heart thumping when he realized that he had a chance of winning now — if only he didn't fall himself.

And so he kept it simple, doing a straight but very

high and smooth jump. By not taking any chances, he was daring Riley to catch up by taking more and more risks of falling.

"Gutless," Riley commented after Matt's third jump. "What a wimp."

Matt laughed off his comment. "Whatever," he said. "Your turn."

"Oh, no," Riley said, wagging his finger. "You go first the rest of the way."

Matt shrugged. "Sure," he said, pushing off and heading for the starting line.

"And let's see a little something!" Riley said. "No wimping out!"

Part of Matt wanted to respond by doing a 360 turn, just to show Riley he was no wimp. But he'd been sucked in once that morning when he accepted Riley's challenge in the first place. He knew Riley was just trying to goad him into failing, that it was a trap designed to make him mess up. So he stayed simple, doing a little zigzag in midair with his board and taking no major chances.

Maybe it was Riley's taunting, but Nelson, Abby, Courtney, and the three other kids acting as judges gave Matt sevens and eights. Melissa voted last, and as she hesitated, he could tell she wanted to give him a higher number — maybe a nine — but she didn't want to stand out too much, so she said "seven" instead.

"Okay," Riley said, energized by Matt's low tally. "Here we go." He launched into his fourth jump, did a 360 turn, and made a perfect landing. Then he thrust both fists high in the air. "Yes! I rule! Give it up, you guys! That was a ten!"

The judges agreed. Not one kid gave him anything less than a ten.

Matt couldn't figure out where he and Riley stood with one jump left to go, but Courtney had been keeping score on a candy box with a little pencil she had in her pocket. "Matt's ahead, 254 to 248," she said. "Close!"

"Ooo-ooo!" some of the kids said, getting a kick out of the tense match.

It was time for Matt's last jump, and he knew that he had to do something special or risk losing. He wanted to beat Riley Hammett at his own game — just to teach him a lesson, just to show him that he wasn't as big a cheese as he thought he was.

It was time for his own 360, he decided. He would risk it all on this one big jump. Taking a deep breath and blowing it out, he closed his eyes for a moment and tried to visualize what he was about to do.

Then he began his jump, holding back till the last minute before springing into a full extension just as his board left the ground. He twisted hard left with his upper torso, forcing the rest of him to follow around in a complete circle. As he came around front again, he tried to hold the fall line of the hill in his sights and point the front of his board straight down it. He spread his arms to his sides and landed softly, with only a little wobble.

He didn't even hear the whoop that went up from the kids at the top of the ramp, but he knew it from the way they were jumping up and down and clapping. He knew he had put Riley Hammett on the spot — big-time.

Riley was silent, concentrated, still as a statue for a long, long moment. Then he made his jump — a 360, like Matt's. It was higher than Matt's and longer to the landing. But Riley's landing was anything but smooth. He nearly fell down and had to touch the ground with his left hand in order to not go over.

The applause from the top of the ramp was polite

but nervous. Matt got on the lift along with Riley, and they rode back up to find out what the final tally was.

"Nine," Nelson was saying as they approached the group.

"Ten," Abby said.

"Ten," Courtney echoed. Riley went over to her and Abby and threw an arm around each of their shoulders.

"What are you talking about?" Melissa said hotly. "Didn't you even see it? I give it a four, and that's being generous!"

The three other judges, two boys and a girl, looked at each other furtively. "Ten," said one.

"Nine," said the second.

"Nine," said the third.

Courtney was hard at work with her pencil and paper. "Riley wins by three points!" she squealed. "Yay!"

The kids all mobbed Riley, who accepted their congratulations with hugs and backslaps and high-fives.

"You were robbed," Melissa told Matt, who stood there stony-faced. "Courtney, let me see that scorecard."

"What, don't you trust me?" Courtney asked, handing it over. "You think I'd cheat?"

"Oh, what's the point?" Melissa said, handing it back without even checking it. "This was so fixed, it's ridiculous." She gave Riley a hard look. "And everybody at school's going to know it, too."

"What?" Riley said, his brows furrowing. "What do you mean by that?"

"Nothing," she said. "Come on, Matt. Let's go have some fun for a change."

Matt followed her, barely waving goodbye to the others.

He had just been given a graphic illustration of how things worked around here. This was Riley Hammett's world, and there was no place in it for him. No place, that is, except at the very bottom of the pile.

7

Hey, hey!" Spengler greeted him on the bus Monday morning. "I hear you're the new snowboard king!" He gave Matt an elaborate handshake with his good arm.

Matt snorted. "Where'd you hear that?"

"It's all over town," Spengler said. "The phones have been busy all night. It's not every day someone out-boards Riley Hammett."

"He won, or didn't they tell you that?" Matt asked.

"He did? That's not the way I heard it."

"Yeah, well, trust me. I was there," Matt said.

"I heard you made him look silly," Spengler insisted.

What is it with this town? Matt wondered. Didn't these kids have anything better to do than to talk about him? He guessed that most of them were bored a lot of the time, and that a new kid from the big city seemed interesting and mysterious. But still, he was just a kid like the rest of them. Why did they have to make such a big deal about him?

Matt decided to change the subject. "Hey, Spengler," he said, "how come everyone's always talking trash about you?"

"You mean like, what did I do to deserve it?" Spengler asked.

"No. Well, yeah," Matt said.

Spengler frowned. "I used to be popular, kind of," he said. "Back in sixth grade. But you know, stuff happens. . . ." He fell silent, and Matt could see a great sadness in his eyes.

He was sorry now that he'd pressed Spengler so hard. He hated bumming people out. There was already too much misery in the world. "Hey, man, forget it," he said. "How's the arm doing?"

"It itches," Spengler complained, but Matt could see the dark cloud lift from his mood. "When the cast comes off, the first thing I'm gonna do is scratch my arm till it bleeds."

"Eeeuw!" Matt said, reacting with a wince. He was glad when the bus pulled up in front of the school. He liked Spengler, but the other kids were right about one thing — he was weird. The things he said were never what you'd expect.

In fact, the day was full of unexpected occurrences. Perkins greeted him in the hallway with a big high-five and asked him if he wanted to work on the school newspaper. "All the cool kids are on the staff," he said.

"Uh, no thanks," Matt replied. "Newspaper reporting really isn't my thing." He wasn't wild about working after school hours, but more to the point, he wondered what Perkins was thinking. Since Matt had started school, Perkins hadn't said two words to him. Now, all of the sudden, he was his best buddy.

Then in homeroom, Melissa passed him a note that read, "Meet me outside the front doors after lunch period. I have to talk to you."

He stuffed the note in his pocket and tried to concentrate on schoolwork the rest of the morning. At lunch, he didn't see Melissa, but Riley and his friends were in their usual seats. They all gave Matt hostile glances, leading Matt to wonder how they'd be acting toward him if he'd been pronounced the winner of the contest. He could only imagine.

He hunkered down at a table by himself and picked

up his fork. But he could only eat a few bites. His stomach was in knots, and he couldn't help wondering what Melissa wanted to talk to him about. Halfway through the period, he went out into the deserted hallway and, when no one was around, sneaked outside.

It was a warm day for January, but Matt didn't have his jacket, and the cold air cut right through the thin fabric of his shirt. Why had she insisted on meeting him outside? And where *was* she, anyway?

He was already shivering. He wished he'd stopped at his locker to grab his coat first. He tried the door, but it was locked from the inside! Great. He'd have to go all the way around to the front and hope no one saw him coming back in. Being outside during school was strictly against the rules, he knew.

The door opened suddenly, and Matt felt a wave of relief come over him. But it wasn't Melissa. It was Spengler. "Hey, mon!" he greeted Matt. "Wuzzup? You look like you just saw a ghost."

"I thought you were someone else," Matt confessed. "I was supposed to meet her out here."

"Her?"

"Melissa McCarthney."

"Oh, man! She's a babe. You two going out?"

"Not really. She wanted to tell me something, that's all."

"Man, she went home after second period."

"What?"

"Yeah, she had a fever or something. She went to the nurse's office, and they sent her home." He laughed. "That stinks for you."

"Yeah." Matt was really shivering now. "What are *you* doing out here?" he asked.

"I needed a mental-health break," Spengler said, sitting on the top step and fishing in his backpack for something. "Ah, here we go." To Matt's astonishment, he pulled out a pack of cigarettes. "Want one?"

"No way," Matt said, waving him off. "That stuff'll kill you."

"Yeah. well, we're all gonna die someday," Spengler said, trying to take a cigarette out of the pack with his one good hand. "Hey, help me out here, would you?"

Matt felt guilty helping Spengler damage his health, but he didn't want to make an issue of it. With shivering hands, he took the pack from him and removed a cigarette.

Spengler had fished a lighter out of his pocket in the meantime. "Here, would you light me up?"

"No, dude," Matt said. "I'm not gonna be a part of you messing up your health." He stuck the pack back in Spengler's book bag. A bunch of quarters and dimes spilled out, and Matt started picking them up and stuffing them back in. Then he handed Spengler the cigarette. "You ought to quit, man."

"I've tried," Spengler said. "But it's really hard to. Stay away from tobacco, man, I'm telling you."

Matt didn't need to be told. He watched, wincing as Spengler lit up. Then his gaze turned to the window behind them, and he froze.

There was Abby, her eyes wide with shock and surprise — and something else, too. She looked distinctly *happy*. Like a cat that had just spotted a wounded bird.

Matt knew right away there would be trouble. But he could never have guessed how much.

No one saw Matt and Spengler sneak back into the school building. But it seemed like everybody instantly knew Matt had been out there. Kids were whispering about him again. And the compliments and friendliness had stopped. Not one other kid talked to him all afternoon, but he knew everyone was talking *about* him.

When he got home, he called Melissa, but her

mother picked up. She said Melissa had a fever and was sleeping. Matt did his homework, watched TV, and waited for Uncle Clayton to come home from work.

Clay was late today. Maybe he had a big meeting or something. Matt decided to amuse himself by going on the Web and looking for local chat rooms. He found one called Dragontalk. Sure enough, it was a site for kids in the area to talk about whatever was new and exciting.

His name was all over it. "I saw Matt Harper outside school today, smoking with Spengler," said Chika-dee23. Matt knew that had to be Abby.

"Word!?!?!?" said Ugogirl.

"I hear he does drugs," said Perkomeister. Perkins, Matt guessed. His "good buddy" from this morning.

"Did you know Harper's mother is doing time in prison for drug dealing?" said TopDog90.

"No lie?" Perkomeister replied.

Matt stared at the screen in disbelief. He wanted to write a reply of his own, but he knew it would be no use. They'd know it was him, and they'd never believe him anyway.

"Yeah, she's in for twenty years!" TopDog90 wrote.

"That's why he's living with his uncle. I also heard he got kicked out of school in Chicago for gang stuff."

"Gang stuff?" Ugogirl wrote. "What did he do?"

"I didn't do *anything!*" Matt said out loud. "I was never in a gang! I never even *knew* anybody in a gang! And my mom's working for the government, you dweebs!"

But he didn't type anything. He continued to eavesdrop on the conservation.

Chikadee23: "I think he was selling something to Spengler. There was money all over the place."

TopDog90: "He's definitely trouble."

Perkomeister: "*In* trouble, you mean."

Ugogirl: "And he dresses like a gangsta."

TopDog90: "He *is* a gangsta."

Perkomeister: "Somebody better warn Spengler."

Chikadee23: "Somebody better warn *Melissa.*"

Matt slammed his fist down on the desk so hard it hurt. Then he put his fingers on the keys and, throwing caution to the wind, typed, "Where'd you guys hear all this about Harper?"

"Who's here?" TopDog90 wrote. "Who's Claybuilder?"

Matt didn't write back.

"Where *did* you hear it?" Perkomeister wrote.

"Not at liberty to say," TopDog90 wrote back. "Strictly confidential, but definitely a reliable source."

"Yeah," Matt said under his breath. "Your own imagination, Riley."

He was still frowning at the screen when the phone rang.

Uncle Clayton appeared in his room, holding the receiver. "It's for you."

Now what?

"Who is it?" Matt asked.

"I don't know, but she sounds pretty," Clay said with a twinkle in his eye.

Matt took the phone. "Hello?"

"Hi, it's me. Melissa."

"Oh, hi. How're you feeling?"

"Better, thanks. Sorry I didn't stay around to meet you."

"I wish you had," Matt said. "I think I got myself in trouble."

"What happened?"

"Nothing happened," he insisted. "But I might be in

trouble anyway. People are saying I was smoking at school."

"But you didn't?"

"No. I swear. I don't even smoke!" He sighed. "I just hope they don't call me into the principal's office."

"If they do, just tell the truth," she advised him. "You've never been in any trouble before, right? I'm sure they'll believe you."

"Yeah. I guess so."

But he *had* been in trouble before. And his school records would show it. They would tell how, in sixth grade, he'd forged an excuse note, stayed out of school, and gone to see his dad in a futile attempt to get him to come back home.

They would tell, too, about the fight he'd had last year with that racist kid who'd been picking on his Pakistani friend Ameer. The kid had been bigger than Matt, but he'd fought him anyway, and although he got a bloody nose and a black eye for his trouble, Matt wasn't sorry about it.

It was terrible, he thought, *how even little mistakes could count against you the next time you messed up.* And what had he done, really? Just given Spengler one of his own cigarettes. That was bad enough, but somehow, it had gotten blown out of all proportion.

Maybe the school would let me off the hook this time, he thought hopefully. But probably not.

He said good-bye, sighed, and hung up the phone.

"Everything all right?" Clay asked, concerned.

"Yeah," Matt said glumly. "Everything's peachy."

"Come on," Clay said. "Who do you think you're talking to?"

"Sorry," Matt said sincerely. "It's just . . . school problems."

"Wanna talk about it?"

"Not right now. Maybe tomorrow." There'd be time enough to talk about it then, Matt figured. *If* he got reported to the principal. If he didn't, there was no point in telling Uncle Clayton about it.

Or was there?

Why, oh, why, did his mom have to go away?

Matt went up to bed early, feeling sorrier for himself than he'd ever felt in his life.

8

The next day at school, most kids seemed to give him a wide berth. Even Melissa eyed him warily.

"What's wrong?" he asked her in the hallway after homeroom.

"You lied to me last night."

"I did not! I swear, I didn't smoke!"

"You were *seen*, Matt. Caught red-handed."

"By who? By Abby?"

Melissa didn't answer.

"She's lying," he insisted. "Or maybe she just *thought* she saw me smoking."

"Huh?" Melissa looked extremely skeptical.

"Spengler asked me to fish a cigarette out of his backpack for him," Matt explained. "You know, his cast and all? And then he asked me to light it for him."

Melissa seemed to consider this. "You'd better not be lying to me."

"I'm not!"

She shook her head slowly, looking disappointed in him. "Whatever," she said. "If you say so. Look, I've gotta go to class."

"See you later, okay?" he asked.

She had already started down the hallway, but he saw her shrug without turning. Maybe she would and maybe she wouldn't, the shrug seemed to say. But one thing was for sure — she didn't really believe him, even after he'd told her the whole story. Which meant that Abby must have been a very convincing "eyewitness."

Great.

Things got worse quickly. In the middle of first period, he was called down to the principal's office. When he opened the door, Spengler was already sitting there, staring miserably into space. He looked up at Matt and gave him a weak smile. "Looks like we got ourselves into some trouble," he said.

"*We?*" Matt replied.

He would have said more, but the principal came in at that moment. He sat down, stared across his desk at them, and began talking.

"As I'm sure you know, Mr. Spengler, this school has a zero-tolerance policy regarding smoking on school grounds."

Spengler nodded and stared at the floor between his feet.

"Mr. Harper, you're new here, I recognize that, and perhaps you aren't acquainted with some of the school's lesser-known rules. The no-smoking rule is three strikes and you're out. Mr. Spengler," he said, turning away from Matt, "this is your second offense. One more, and you're suspended for three days. I hope it's the last time I see you here for this offense."

"Oh, it will be, Mr. Koppel," Spengler assured him in an innocent tone Matt had never heard him use before.

"I'm going to bend the rules for you, Mr. Harper, because you're new here. I'll let you off the hook this time."

"Thanks, Mr. Koppel," Matt said, feeling a wave of relief flood over him. He wanted to say it wouldn't happen again, but the fact was, it hadn't even happened *this* time! Of course, if he said that — if he protested his innocence — he might bring down a harsher punishment. So he decided to just go with the flow. What had Uncle Clayton said? "You have to go along to get along."

"But next time, you will be suspended, understood?"

"Understood," Matt said.

"Good." The principal got up. "You may go back to your classes, gentlemen."

As Spengler stood, he gave Matt a little nod and mouthed the words, *Only one more and I'm free!*

He'd actually be happy to get a three-day suspension, Matt realized with a start.

Matt would definitely not have been happy. He'd been suspended after the fight back in Chicago, and he knew that a suspension was more than a free vacation. It went down on your record and followed you all through your school life. You were marked as a "bad kid" and watched over like a hawk. Matt wondered if Principal Koppel had access to his old school records. Probably. But had he even looked through them? Probably not. Lucky for Matt, too.

"Oh, Mr. Harper," the principal said, stopping him as he was about to leave.

"Yes?"

"You do understand, of course, that we'll have to call home to notify your family about this incident."

"What?" A sudden surge of alarm rose through Matt's body.

"That's a school policy I can't bend on, I'm afraid." The principal sat back down at his desk. "You may go now."

Matt left and headed for his second period class. Uncle Clayton would understand, he knew. He'd definitely believe Matt hadn't been smoking. But would he tell Matt's mom next time she called? That would be *really* terrible.

Lunchtime was so bad that he felt like bagging it altogether, going without food and spending the period in the library, where he wouldn't have to talk to anyone. But he was hungry, and he'd never been good at fasting. So he took a deep breath and entered the cafeteria.

The loud noise of dozens of conversations suddenly dropped to murmurs. This time, not just Riley's table but *all* the tables were focused on nothing but him. He got in the food line and ignored the questions from the curious kids surrounding him, most of whom were sixth and seventh graders.

"Were you really in juvie?"

"What was it like?"

"What kinds of drugs was your mom dealing?"

"What gang were you in?"

Finally, Matt couldn't take it anymore. "SHUT UP!" he exploded. "Just — just shut up, all of you! Okay?"

They did, but that just made him feel worse. After all, these were just a bunch of curious kids. They didn't have anything against him, really, and he could tell he had really scared them.

Well, better that than listening to their stupid questions, he thought. He paid for his food, then stalked off to the far corner of the cafeteria and sat at a table tucked behind a big pillar where no one could see him.

His mind was working a mile a minute. Maybe he should call up his dad and stepmom and say he wanted to move in with them after all. Bad as he knew it would be, it couldn't be worse than Dragon Valley had been so far. Even living with those three little brats day in, day out . . . hmmm . . . on second thought, maybe that wasn't such a good idea.

Or he could go off to a boarding school, like his mom had suggested. But that might wind up being just like here, without Uncle Clayton to take care of him and without a great mountain to snowboard on.

His sandwich felt like lumps of paste going down his throat, and no amount of apple juice would help it go down easier. No, he was going to have to stay here and stick it out, no matter how much it hurt or how much of a school outcast he became.

Thinking about outcasts reminded him of Spengler. It was Spengler who'd gotten him into this mess in the first place. If he hadn't sat at the back of that stupid bus that first day, none of this would have happened. He'd have made friends with the popular kids, like Riley and the others. But no, he had to go sit next to Spengler, and ever since, he'd been lumped in with him in everyone's mind.

And why had he ignored Riley's advice to stay away from Melissa? If he hadn't gone snowboarding with her that day, Riley wouldn't have challenged him to that contest. He wouldn't have made a fool of the most popular kid in the whole school — and no one would have cared that he was outside with Spengler instead of in class. No one would have been spreading rumors about him all over the Internet and turning him in to the principal. And then, right when he needed a friend, Melissa had turned on him, too.

He hated Melissa, he decided, almost as much as he hated Spengler, and even more than he hated his mom for doing this to him.

In fact, Matt decided, he hated *everybody*.

Shoving aside his mostly uneaten lunch, he got up and left the cafeteria. The period was almost over anyway, and he didn't feel like killing time in there with all those kids talking about him.

He was walking past the big bulletin board by the school's front entrance. All kinds of notices were posted here: announcements for meetings of various clubs and after-school activities, stuff about the science fair in February, calls for volunteers at the local animal shelter and food pantry.

Then his eyes fell on a yellow poster he hadn't seen before. The words SNOWBOARD CONTEST caught his attention, and he wandered over to take a closer look.

"Snowboard contest, Saturday, February 1, open to all students age 11–14," the poster read. "Girls and boys. Jumps and half-pipe competitions. First prize in each category — a new top-of-the-line snowboard AND complete outfit, including parka, gloves, boots, hat, and goggles. Proceeds to benefit Dragon Valley Home/School Association. Enter by signing up below." And at the bottom of the poster was a place with horizontal lines for filling in your name.

There were no names filled in yet. The poster must have been put up just minutes ago, because in this school, Matt knew, there were dozens of kids who would be thrilled to enter. Matt took out his pen and bent over to sign his name on the first line.

"Don't bother, loser."

Matt hadn't heard Riley approach. At the sound of Riley's voice in his ear, he'd let out a little scared sound.

Now Riley was laughing at him. "You *should* be scared," he said. "This competition is no competition at all. I am the snowboard king, man. Didn't I already beat you once? You know you're just wasting your time."

Matt didn't respond to Riley's taunts. Instead, he said, "I know you told everyone I smoked on school grounds."

"Not that I'm admitting anything, but what if I did? It's true, isn't it?"

"No," Matt said. "But that's not the point. You shouldn't be spreading rumors, true or false. And in fact, I happen to know you've been making up a lot of stuff about me."

"What if I have?" Riley said, standing his ground. "You wanna make something of it?"

Matt could have punched him right there. Even though Riley was bigger and looked stronger, Matt knew he could do some damage in a fight. But what would that accomplish? He'd only get himself suspended or even expelled! He could just hear Riley laughing if that happened. So he backed off, forcing himself to stay calm.

"I didn't smoke."

"Yeah, right."

"Ask Spengler."

"Spengler? Ha! That's a good one. That kid's a total burnout. Has he even attended class this year?"

"Hey, maybe he has real problems," Matt said, rising to Spengler's defense even though just minutes before he'd been filled with hatred for the social outcast.

"No, ya think?" Riley said, laughing.

"You shouldn't make fun of people's problems," Matt said. "Maybe you don't think you have problems yourself, but take my word for it, you do."

Riley glared at him. "You know what my problem is?" he said. "It's *you*. But don't worry. I know how to deal with problems."

"Oh, yeah? How?"

"You'll see," Riley said. Leaning past Matt, he signed his name on the first line.

Matt waited till he was done, then signed his own name right under Riley's.

"So be it," Riley said, staring at him. "Just remember, you asked for it."

"Asked for what?" Matt asked.

"Like I said, you'll see." Riley turned and walked away.

Matt watched him go with a sinking feeling in his stomach. Five minutes ago, he would have bet that his life couldn't get any worse than it already was. Now he knew better. It was going to get a whole lot worse.

9

That night, just before he was about to go to bed, there was a knock on Matt's door. "Hey, can I come in for a minute?" Uncle Clayton asked.

"Sure," Matt said.

"Hey," Clay said, opening the door and sitting in the chair by Matt's desk. "How's it going?"

"Okay. What's up?" Matt asked.

"I just got the feeling we should talk," Clay said. "You seem like you've got a lot on your mind. I've kind of let things go along because I was busy. But I'm starting to feel like a bad parent."

"You're not my parent," Matt pointed out — not trying to be unkind, just stating the truth.

"I know, but I'm supposed to be watching out for you, and I guess I haven't been." He paused again, waiting. Then he said, "Something's up, isn't it? I mean, there's something wrong, right? I mean —"

Matt stopped him. "Yeah. There is."

"I knew it," Clay said. "But what? You can't talk about it with me?"

"No, I can," Matt said, "It's just . . . I don't know. There's this kid at school, and he's making life pretty tough for me."

"I'll tell him to cut it out," Clay offered. "You want me to?"

"No," Matt said. "Thanks, but it's not that kind of thing. He's just . . . I guess he feels threatened by me or something."

"In what way?"

"Well, there's this girl he likes who likes me. . . ."

"Aha!" Clay said, perking up.

"But there's more to it than that. I crashed into him on the slopes, and then he challenged me to a contest, and I beat him, but he won. . . ."

"Huh? How's that?"

"His friends voted him the winner, but it was an obvious fix. I kind of made him look bad, and now he's trying to get me into trouble."

"Ah. Would that explain the message I had from the principal today?"

Matt gulped. "Yeah. This kid reported me for smoking on school grounds."

"Smoking? You?"

"I wasn't," Matt explained hurriedly. "There's this kid with a broken arm, and he asked me to light his cigarette for him, and someone saw me do it. . . ."

"That was pretty dumb of you," Clay said. "And now the principal's going to be watching you. One more mistake and . . ."

"I know," Matt said glumly.

"Your mom's gonna throw a fit. She's gonna blame me for not taking good care of you."

"She doesn't have to know, does she?" Matt asked, a pleading look in his eyes.

Clay didn't answer right away. Then he said, "Tell you what. I'll hold off for a bit, but only if you work on turning things around. Otherwise, I really do have to tell her."

"It's a deal," Matt said gratefully. "And I might already have figured out a way to make people see me for who I really am — and see Riley for who he really is. There's going to be a half-pipe and jumping contest

94

sponsored by the school. I signed up, and so did he. He's famous for being the best boarder in the whole school. Maybe if I beat him in the contest, people will see me differently."

Clay cocked his head to one side. "How do you figure?"

"Okay, this may sound a little lame, but if I've learned anything about the kids at this school, it's that they pay attention to whoever is snowboard champ. If I win, maybe they'll listen to my side of the story. Who knows, maybe they'll even realize that Riley isn't so great after all. Only trouble is, I'm not sure I can beat him."

"Well, if that's the best plan you've got, I'll help you make it happen," Clay said, slapping his hands together. "I'm gonna work with you, pal — and you're gonna take over that title!"

Matt couldn't deny that he liked that idea. Uncle Clayton could teach him some awesome jumps and tricks. Still, he'd just realized there was one major problem with his plan. "If I beat this kid, he'll just make my life miserable."

Clay shook his head. "Uh-uh. You said it yourself! Once you beat him, *you'll* be the big cheese around the school, not him. I know how it works. I was a kid here once myself, and not too long ago, either. If he talks trash about you, kids will just think he's jealous. And they'll be right, too."

It wasn't much to go on, but at least it was something to hold on to, a hope that things could be better for him here in Dragon Valley.

The next day was Saturday, and Clay took Matt out on the slopes of Dragon Mountain. They started at the jump ramps, where Matt showed his uncle everything he knew how to do — which, he came to see, wasn't that much.

Clay gave him pointers after every jump: "You need to hit the jump a little faster and ollie as you get to the top," he advised. And after another run: "Make sure your board isn't on an edge at takeoff. That makes you lose your balance in the air."

Clay didn't feel that Matt needed that many jumps. "You can do a lot of variations with the same few basic moves," he said, demonstrating for Matt a few times and getting wows from everyone nearby.

So Matt practiced his few jumps. Once he was consistently hitting them, Clay began adding flourishes: "We're gonna do a little chicken salad," he said.

"Chicken salad?" Matt repeated, laughing.

"Your front hand grabs between your feet and through your legs," he explained. "To the heel edge. That's right," he added as Matt tried to go through the move while standing still.

Matt could feel himself getting better by the moment. With Uncle Clayton behind him, he would soon be super-skilled physically and super-confident mentally. He smiled at the thought. This contest was going to be no contest at all. He was going to blow Riley Hammett right off the mountain.

On Sunday, they hit the slopes again. "I should've spent more time with you from the beginning," Clay said apologetically, as they rode the lift together to the top of the half-pipe. "You wouldn't have gotten yourself into this mess in the first place if I'd been on the job."

"That's okay, Uncle Clayton," Matt said. "I mean, you've got a life, too. You're not my dad, after all, and besides, I should be able to take care of myself by now."

Clay patted him on the head affectionately. "Yeah," he said, "but you shouldn't have to."

They made their way to the top of the half-pipe. "I haven't done the half-pipe since last year," Matt said nervously.

"Don't try to get air the first time down," Clay advised him. "Just give yourself a nice smooth trip. Get the feel of the pipe. Smooth through the transitions. Then, as you feel more comfortable, you can take some air and even try a few grabs."

Clay's approach was great for confidence building. Matt tried things over and over until he had them down, then added a little bit of flourish or extension when he was ready. He could feel himself improving run by run.

After lunch, it was back to the jumps.

"I think we'll try a little roast beef now," Clay said, as they rode up the mountain.

"I've heard of that move," Matt replied. "It's the flip side of the chicken salad, right?"

"Right. Same grab, but with the back hand instead of the front. Yeah, roast beef and chicken salad — and we're gonna bone it, too."

"Bone it?"

"Yeah. It's stylin', y'know? You straighten one leg while you're in the air and hold it till just before you land."

Matt listened to every word his uncle told him. He listened in a way he never listened to a teacher in a classroom. When he'd first moved in with Clay, he'd liked snowboarding a lot. Now it was his passion — and this contest was going to be a defining moment in his life, he could just feel it.

Snowboard Champ lurked in the trees at the top of the mountain, waiting for his quarry to appear. The bank robbers had gotten away clean with the cash, riding off in their commandeered helicopter. The chopper would drop them here at the top of the mountain, where they would snowboard down to their underground cavern hideout. Only they had no idea he was here, ready to foil their plans. . . .

The whir of the rotors alerted him to the chopper's approach. There! It was letting off its passengers, loaded with the precious cargo stowed in the backpacks they wore.

Here they came, down the hill toward him. He let them pass him, then shoved off in hot pursuit. He carved a path almost directly down the fall line, cutting in front of the robbers one after the other, startling them, and causing them to tumble head over heels down the mountain. And when they stopped tumbling, he was there waiting for them, nylon handcuffs at the ready.

When they were safely hog-tied, he radioed back to base. "Quarry captured," he said. "Send the police choppers in."

"Good work, Snowboard Champ," the voice on the other end crackled. "How in the world did you do it?"

He smiled under his red and black mask and goggles. "Just . . . lucky, I guess."

Monday morning dawned, a bright, cold, sunny day, and Matt got on the bus to school in a good mood. Spengler was back at the rear of the bus, and Matt joined him readily. There was a bounce in his step as he walked down the aisle of the bus.

Matt didn't care anymore if people thought he was a troublemaker. Soon he'd be the king of the hill at Dragon Valley Middle. And just as soon as the contest was over and he was judged the runaway winner, he'd show them just how wrong they were about him.

He sat down next to Spengler, who looked surprised. "Hi!" he said.

"Hi."

"I thought you might not be speaking to me after what happened last week."

Matt elbowed Spengler in his good arm. "I was mad at first," he admitted. "But I realized it wasn't your fault."

"I'm quitting, by the way. Smoking, I mean."

"That's cool. Good move."

"Hey, my cast's coming off next week."

"Oh, yeah?" Good."

"So I can punch out whoever turned us in."

"Whoa," Matt said. "Go easy, okay? We're in enough trouble already."

"It'll be on me," Spengler said. "What do you care?"

Matt looked at him long and hard. "What *is* it with you?" he asked. Then, softly, so no one else could hear, "Hey, Spengler — how'd you break your arm?"

Spengler stared out the window.

"I won't tell anyone," Matt said. "You can trust me."

"It's not true, what they're saying," Spengler told him. "About my dad breaking my arm. It's not true."

"Okay. I believe you. So what *did* happen?"

Spengler sniffed, and Matt leaned in toward him so the other kids on the bus wouldn't hear them.

"I hit it against a brick wall."

Matt flinched. "On purpose?"

"Yeah. On account of my dad kept screaming at my

101

mom. I had to hit something. I figured, better a wall than a person."

"Whoa . . . man . . ."

Remembering the jokes those other kids had told about Spengler and how he'd broken his arm, Matt felt sick to his stomach. Here was a kid with *real* problems — while their only problem was who to trash next.

Matt was so angry that, like Spengler, he could have punched a wall right then and there. But no — he had a better way to shut those kids up. When he won this competition and became the coolest kid at Dragon Valley Middle, he would set a different tone.

The bus arrived at school. From the moment he stepped onto the sidewalk, Matt knew that today would be no ordinary day.

In front of the school, a crowd of kids was gathered. They were staring at something on the wall, but they were blocking the view and Matt couldn't see past them. When he did work his way through them and saw what they were looking at, he froze.

Written on the wall, in bright, spray-painted colors, was a graffiti tag. It read:

Chicago Dukes.

As he stared at the writing, he heard someone mutter, "That's him over there. He's the one who did it." He didn't have to look up to know the kid was talking about him.

10

The crowd parted like the Red Sea on either side of Matt. *"What?"* he asked them. "Hey, it wasn't me! I swear!"

It wasn't working. No one looked convinced. Feeling a surge of panic rising inside him, Matt ran up the steps and into the school building. He kept running until he found the boys' bathroom. Inside, he went into a stall, locked it, and stood there, leaning against the door, trying to catch his breath.

This couldn't be happening! He couldn't believe Riley Hammett would go this far. But there were the words on the wall, and whoever had sprayed them up there obviously meant for people to think it was Matt — the new boy from Chicago, rumored to be a gangsta, with a mother in prison for dealing drugs.

Of course it had been Riley. Who else would have

done something like that? Besides, it fit the pattern. First the rumors, now the actual bad stuff, all aimed at making Matt out to be a troublemaker.

But *why?* Why would anyone do such a thing? Why would someone go so far as to hurt somebody that never hurt him?

One thing was for sure — Matt was hurting now. He could feel all the confidence he'd built up in the past two days draining out of him.

He'd been kidding himself. Did he really think he could upset the whole social order? He was just the new kid in town. First you're curious about him. He's mysterious and cool. Then you realize he's different, and you toss him in the bin with the other outcasts.

That was what would happen to him. He'd be permanently grouped with the Spenglers of this world. Well, so be it. *Better Spengler than them,* he thought. At least Spengler never did anything mean to anybody.

No, Matt thought miserably. *Spengler only did hurtful things to himself.*

He took one more deep breath, steadied himself, and opened the stall door. He stared into a mirror, not sure if he looked okay or not. Was that fear showing in his eyes?

He went out into the hallway, and the first person he saw was Melissa. He'd almost forgotten about her ever since the contest had come up. She hadn't called him, either, and he fully expected her to turn her back on him now as she had before. But to his surprise, she hurried over to him.

"Hi," she said.

"Hi," he said back.

"I was gonna call you . . . ," she began.

"Yeah?"

"But I was mad busy this weekend."

"That's okay. So was I," Matt was quick to say.

There was a wall between them that had not been there before. It was invisible, but Matt could feel it. *A wall of ice.* She still had her doubts about him — and now, he had his doubts about *her,* too.

He went off to class, but he knew it would only be a matter of time until he was called down to the principal's office. When second period began, though, and he still hadn't been called in, he began to relax. Maybe it *wouldn't* happen. After all, nobody could prove it was him.

A chill came over him then. Maybe someone *would* say they'd seen him. One of Riley's friends. They'd lied about the cigarette, hadn't they? Of course, that could have been a misunderstanding, perhaps even an honest mistake. He'd had a cigarette in his hand, after all. But if someone would spray graffiti and make it look like it was him, they might also lie and say they saw him do it.

By the middle of third period, he could stand the tension no longer. He asked the teacher to be excused, and she gave him a bathroom pass. He was on his way down the hall when he saw Riley coming toward him. He was with two other students and the chemistry teacher, Mr. Bonom. They were carrying beakers and talking about their experiment. They paid no attention to Matt as they passed. But Riley noticed him, all right. Matt saw his eyes flicker as they went by each other.

He'd better not go outside, Matt decided. Where then? The boys' room again. He hoped no one was in there. He needed to collect himself and get ready in his mind to explain things to the principal.

He had no sooner gone in there, however, than the fire alarm went off. The boys' room was next to the main office, and Matt could hear the school secretaries talking outside the door.

"What's going on?" one said. "There wasn't a drill scheduled."

"Somebody must have pulled the alarm," said another.

"I hope there isn't really a fire," the first one said.

"If there isn't, somebody's gonna be in big trouble," the second replied.

Matt's heart sank. He knew in his heart what had just happened, even though he had no proof. He was finished here in Dragon Valley. It was all over. He had lost the game before it ever got started.

The call came in the middle of fifth period, and Matt was prepared for it. What he wasn't prepared for was the policeman sitting next to the principal.

"Matthew, this is Officer Pinkshaw," the principal said. Officer Pinkshaw had a shaved head and a fat neck and was looking at Matt as if he were a criminal.

"Hi," Matt said, offering his hand. Officer Pinkshaw didn't take it.

"Matthew," he said, "I want you to tell me and the principal the truth now."

"Yessir," Matt agreed. He was sitting down, but he could feel his legs trembling.

"Are you responsible for the graffiti that was sprayed on the school building last night?"

"No!" Matt said much too loudly. "I swear, I had nothing to do with it!"

"Somebody set off a false alarm this morning," the principal went on. "Was that you?"

"NO!"

"I understand you weren't in class at the time the alarm was pulled," said the principal.

"I was in the bathroom!" Matt protested, his voice wavering.

The officer sighed. "Look, son," he said, "I'll be frank with you. Vandalism is a serious offense, especially on public property. This town also has an anti-gang ordinance. And setting off false alarms — well, I don't have to tell you how serious that is. People can get seriously hurt if the fire department is off on a false alarm and can't respond in time to a real fire."

"I know that," Matt said, his voice now a whisper.

"The long and short of it is," the policeman went on, "if you cooperate, things will go a lot better for you."

"I didn't *do* anything!" Matt repeated. "I was home last night. Ask my uncle."

"He should be here any minute," Officer Pinkshaw said, staring right at Matt. Sure enough, at that very moment, in walked Uncle Clayton.

"What in blazes is this all about?" he demanded, his face red and his eyes bulging. Matt had seen Uncle Clayton angry once or twice in his life, but never like this.

"Your nephew is under suspicion of vandalism and setting off a false fire alarm." Officer Pinkshaw sounded calm, but Matt could see him tense and put his hand on his club, just in case.

Clay's hands were balled up into fists clutched at his sides. "Matt would never do anything like that," he insisted.

"Maybe you should have a talk with the young man," the principal suggested. "Alone."

"I don't need to talk to him to know that he would never do what you're saying he did," Clay said, leaning over the desk toward the principal. "If you insist on going forward with this, I'll have to hire a lawyer. Do you intend to press charges?"

"We're still investigating," Officer Pinkshaw said. "But —"

"But nothing!" Clay interrupted him. "You've got no proof, and you know it. This is bogus!"

"If you'd like to hire an attorney, that's your prerogative," the officer said, getting up to go. "We'll be in touch with you if and when charges are pending." He looked at Clay and added, "I'd watch that attitude if I were you, sir." He went out with Clay glaring after him, looking like he was about to explode.

"Why don't you sit down?" the principal suggested, offering him a chair.

Clay sat and said, "Look, I'm sorry I lost my temper, but you must see how frustrating this is. I mean, here's a boy who's trying to fit into a new school, with new kids, and has anybody in the school reached out to welcome him? To help him adjust? I got exactly two calls from your office. The first was to verify my address. The second was to tell me my nephew had been given a warning for smoking on school property, when I know for a fact he's never smoked in his life! Does anybody here care at all?"

The principal seemed stung by what Clay had said. "I'm sorry if we've failed your nephew," he said. "But that doesn't excuse what he's done."

"You seem to have your mind made up that it was him," Clay replied. He laid a hand on Matt's shoulder. "I'll tell you something. I'd bet every cent I had — my

111

house, my car, the clothes on my back — that this boy didn't do what you say he did. I've known him longer than you have, and better than you ever will."

"I'm sure you have," the principal said snidely.

"When you've got some proof to show, give me a call," Clay said, getting up. "In the meantime, he's gonna come to school and learn, and he's gonna be in that snowboard competition you're having, and he's gonna win it, too. Come on, Matt. Let's get out of here."

Matt got up to join his uncle. He could have thrown his arms around Clay and hugged him, he was so proud and so grateful to him. Nobody had ever stood up for him that way, especially when it counted so much. He would never forget it. Never.

"I'm afraid not," the principal said, folding his hands in front of him.

"Huh?" Clay said, taken by surprise.

"Matthew won't be taking part in the competition."

"What?" Matt gasped.

No student at this school will participate in any school-sponsored extracurricular activity while he is the subject of a police investigation. That includes our snowboarding contest. I'm sorry."

"B-but —" Clay sputtered.

"There's nothing you can do to change my mind, I'm afraid," the principal said. "The decision is entirely mine, and it is made. Until the young man is cleared of wrongdoing, he will not be a part of any school contest."

Clay swallowed hard, and Matt fought back the tears that were filling his eyes to the brim. "Come on, kid," his uncle said, draping an arm around his shoulder. "We're not wanted here. Let's go home."

11

As bad as things were, this was only the second lowest moment of Matt's life. The day his dad called him into the den and told him he was leaving the family had been even worse.

Still, this was pretty bad. Worse than when his mom had said she was going away for a year. Worse than getting beat up by that gang in the playground when he was eight years old.

Snowboard Champ raced down the mountain, dodging the rocks that were raining down on him from atop the cliffs on either side. Tears stung his face. To think that they thought he was the enemy. If they only knew! He'd been trying to save them from the man-eating space aliens. But they had blamed him for everything. Now they were doomed. Earthling sandwiches in waiting . . .

"Hey, where are we going?" Matt blinked back to reality as Clay turned the car off the main road and through the familiar gates of Dragon Mountain Resort.

"Gonna hit the slopes," Clay said, staring straight ahead.

"Huh?"

"Anger management. Gotta work off some of this rage, dude. I don't know about you, but I'm in need of some ridin'!"

Whatever Matt had expected Clay to do, it hadn't been this. Matt's mom would have scolded him or acted hurt. She'd have assumed he was guilty. So would his dad. But Uncle Clayton was different — and for the first time since he'd come to Dragon Valley, Matt felt like he was in exactly the right place.

They rode the mountain that day until night fell, with no stopping to rest or eat. They rode the black diamond slopes at top speed. It was Matt's first time riding these expert trails, but he had no trouble with them. He was concentrating like he'd never done before in his life. Everything seemed so focused, so automatic.

All his frustrations streamed away behind him, blown by the fierce wind that fired up the slopes and into his face. Whatever tears there were, they froze on his cheeks, and he felt the cold air go down into his lungs like fire.

When they finally went home, they were too exhausted to talk much. But as they pulled into the driveway and Clay turned off the engine, he said, "Matt, you're gonna be in that contest."

"What? How'm I —"

"Not only are you gonna be in it, you're gonna win it."

"But —"

"I don't know how," Clay said, "But I can feel it. Y'know — ESP? You believe in that stuff?"

"I guess," Matt said, not really sure if he did. He hoped Uncle Clayton was right, though.

"Life's not fair a lot of the time," Clay said. "But if there's any justice in this world, you're gonna win that contest."

Matt swallowed hard. "Thanks, Uncle Clayton," he said. "Thanks for sticking up for me."

"*De nada,*" Clay said, sniffing. "Come on, let's get some grub. I'm starving."

School was torture. Before, all the kids had their eyes on him wherever he went. Now, even the *teachers* were watching him. He felt like a criminal, pointed at, whispered about, mistrusted. He had no friends. Even Melissa steered clear of him. He was Spengler — no, even *lower* than Spengler on the totem pole.

In French, a balled-up piece of paper landed on his desk, then rolled into his lap. He picked it up and opened it. It read, "R-U-OK?"

He looked up into Melissa's huge green eyes. He shook his head "no." She bit her bottom lip, obviously feeling sorry for him, and he suddenly couldn't look at her anymore. He didn't want her pity. He didn't want *anyone's* pity.

At lunch, he couldn't bear the cafeteria scene, so he went down the main hallway toward the library — a quiet place to kill time, where no one would bother him. A place where he could even get his homework done, so he'd have the whole late afternoon and evening to go boarding again.

Being on his snowboard had become Matt's only refuge, the only place in his life, aside from his daydreams, where he felt like a hero and not a zero.

"Will Matthew Harper please come to the main office?" the voice on the loudspeaker said. "Matthew Harper to the main office. Thank you."

Uh-oh. Now what?

He pictured the widened eyes and whispers in the cafeteria as his name came over the loudspeaker yet again. He walked out of the library and trudged down the hall like he was on a death march.

"The principal wants to see you," said Mrs. Harrison, the guidance counselor. "Have a seat on the bench over there."

Matt did as he was told and waited for the grim door to open and the bony finger to beckon him inside. Obviously, something else bad had happened and he was being blamed again.

The door finally opened, and the principal's face appeared. "Would you come in here, Matthew?"

Matt rose and put one foot in front of the other until he got to the doorway. Inside, to his surprise, he saw Spengler sitting with a woman who could only have been his mother.

"Sit down," the principal said, indicating an empty chair. Matt sat.

The principal went behind his desk and sat back down, then leaned forward toward Matt and folded his hands in front of him. "Apparently, there's been a mistake. I'm afraid we may have been too hasty in our treatment of you, young man." He glanced at Spengler and his mother, then back at Matt. "Mr. Spengler here says he saw you in the boys' room at the time the fire alarm was pulled and that you didn't do it."

"Spengler?" Matt turned and gave him a grateful look. Spengler gave him a wan smile in return.

But *Spengler?* Why had they believed *him,* a kid like that with a record like his?

As if he'd heard him ask, the principal said, "Mrs. Spengler was with him at the time, and she corroborates his story. They were . . . ahem . . . on their way to this office."

Now Matt understood. The school must have asked Mrs. Spengler to come in for a meeting with the principal, and somehow they'd seen him at the crucial moment.

With all the bad breaks he'd had in his life, here for a change was a really good one! Matt exhaled for what felt like the first time in days.

Then something else occurred to him, something very important. "Does this mean I can be in the snowboarding contest?" he asked.

The principal frowned. "The graffiti incident still casts a shadow over your record, I'm afraid. However, in light of the fact that we've judged you wrongly once,

I'm willing to believe it could be possible we're wrong about that as well. For now, in the absence of further proof, I'll agree to let you participate."

"YES!" Matt yelled, jumping right out of his chair. "Thanks, Mr. Koppel! Thanks, Spengler! Thanks, Spengler's mom!"

The principal was smiling now. "Good. I'm glad we've worked this out. And Mr. Harper . . ."

"Yes?"

"Please convey my apologies to your uncle, will you? I'm sorry we had to drag him in here."

"Okay." Matt thought it would have been better for the principal to say so himself, straight to Uncle Clayton's face if possible. But at the moment, he didn't want to argue. He'd gotten what he wanted. He was back in the contest!

Now the only thing to do was *win* it.

So he and Clay practiced on the half-pipe every minute they could. They practiced on the jumps. And they talked over the mental preparation part, over and over again. "Remember," Clay said, "you're not competing against the other boarders. You're competing against the mountain. I've seen what you've got, dude. If you nail your landings, you're gonna win this thing."

"You really think so?"

"Are you kidding? Snowboarding talent runs in the family."

They worked on his jumps and half-pipe runs every day after school. Twice, they saw Riley. Whenever they did, Matt would bag whatever he was doing. "Come on, Uncle Clayton, let's go do some downhill."

They'd go off where Riley wasn't and wait till next time to practice. Matt didn't want Riley to realize how good his competition was getting. Luckily, and surprisingly, Riley only showed up those two times. Matt, who was there constantly, with and without his uncle, would have known if Riley had come to practice more often. Apparently, Riley was feeling pretty good about his chances.

Matt smiled at the thought. Wait till Riley ran into Snowboard Champ!

The letter from his mom came the afternoon before the contest. He didn't open it. He needed to concentrate on the contest for one more day, and he was afraid whatever was in the letter would upset him, or at least distract him.

But he couldn't stop thinking about it all evening, and even lying in bed that night. Time after time,

Uncle Clayton had told him that focus and concentration were everything in snowboarding. How was he supposed to concentrate when all he could think about was what might be in that letter?

He sat straight up in bed, flicked on his bedside light, and ripped open the envelope, which was postmarked *Karnataka*. Matt thought that was somewhere in India, but he wasn't totally sure.

Dear Matt,

Well, it's been a while since I called, and it will be a while longer till I can call again. I am going to be in small villages with no phones or cellphone towers. I'm taking lots of pictures and keeping a diary so I can remember all the little details to tell you about. Sometime, I hope, I'll be able to bring you here for a visit.

I know I've promised to tell you all about what I'm doing, running all over the world while you're back there — and I hope I hope I hope you're okay and that your uncle is not letting you run totally wild. Anyway, I thought I'd take this opportunity to tell you what I do.

I'm sure it sounds boring, but what I do is called microloans. I represent our government's lending institutions out here in the field, prospecting for opportunities so that people can lift themselves out of poverty by building small businesses. I know it must sound terribly unglamorous, but I find it fascinating and very rewarding.

The other day, I arranged a loan of $100 for this woman to start an egg-production business. All she needed were some chickens, some feed, and the materials to build a chicken coop. And now, with only $100 — the cost of a pair of sneakers in the States! — her family's whole life has been changed. Now they will have some cash in addition to the food that they grow, and they can gradually improve their lives.

I make many loans like this every week, and I love seeing how happy it makes people. If only there were enough money to give everyone that chance! But honey, I do miss you, and I promise that I'll be gone no more than the year I've already committed to. After that, I'll get a post near home, and we'll be together again.

Stay safe, and work hard in school. Love you, baby,

Mom

So. She wasn't a spy after all. Matt had to admit it was a slight disappointment. But thinking about his mom out there in the world, going from place to place spreading opportunity and happiness — well, it was pretty cool, he had to admit. He tucked the letter back into its envelope and stuck it under his pillow. Then he closed his eyes and slept.

Matt awoke when the rising sun, streaming in through the window, hit him square in the eyes. He'd left the shade up on purpose. This was one morning when he didn't want to oversleep. He practically leaped out of bed, he was so eager to get to Dragon Mountain.

Clay was sitting at the kitchen table, sipping some coffee and wolfing down doughnuts. "Want shum?" he asked with his mouth full, pointing to the sugary stuff.

Matt didn't need to be invited twice. At home with his mom, doughnuts were strictly off-limits. Still, as he wolfed down a powdered sugar and a chocolate glazed, he reflected that she was probably right. It was one thing to be a pig at thirteen. But he hoped by the time he turned twenty-seven, he'd have developed better eating habits than Uncle Clayton.

"Let's go!" Matt said, pushing back his chair, getting up, and going to the back of the loft to get his board. He passed the doorway and froze. There, laid out before him, was a display of all-new snowboarding gear — but not just any new gear. The gloves, the helmet, the boots, and the knee and elbow guards were all in lightning bolts of red and black. And on the back of the thin, insulated racing jacket, incredibly, were written the words SNOWBOARD CHAMP.

Matt could not believe his eyes. How had Uncle Clayton known? He couldn't have! Unless . . . "Hey, Uncle Clayton?" he called.

Clay appeared in the doorway behind him, a satisfied look on his face. "Yeah?"

"I can't believe this!"

"Hey, your mom told me to take care of you, right? So? I'm taking care. You've gotta look good when you do good."

"But — Snowboard Champ?" Matt asked.

"You don't like it?" Clay asked. "I just saw it in the store and thought it was kind of 'you,' know what I mean?"

"Oh, it is," Matt said. "It's perfect."

Unbelievable, he thought, *the way life works sometimes.*

They arrived in plenty of time to register for the competition, but there was already a mob of kids there. It almost seemed like every student at Dragon Valley Middle School had entered the contest. Even Spengler was there, broken arm and all.

"Are all these kids in the contest?" Matt asked him.

"Nah. Most of them came to watch — like me. *Baaa . . . baaa.*"

Matt went to check out the list of competitors. In the sixth and seventh grade competitions, there were twelve contestants each. In the eighth grade competition, much to his surprise, there were only four contestants: Jeff Perkins, some girl named Sally Spitzer, Riley Hammett, and Matt.

He guessed nobody else was stupid enough to want to get humiliated by Riley. Oh, well, at least he wasn't the only other person going up against him. He felt a sudden rush of gratitude for Perkins and for Sally Spitzer, whoever she was.

He went over to read the rules and procedures sheet. The three grades would rotate locations. The eighth graders would start on the jumps, then, after a break, compete in the half-pipe. Each sixth and seventh grade contestant got three jumps and two runs down the half-pipe, and the two best riders faced off in a final. For the eighth graders, there were four jumps each and two half-pipe runs. Matt guessed that was due to the lack of contestants.

Okay, so now he knew what he had to prepare. He thought about all the jumps and airs he'd practiced with Uncle Clayton. He couldn't possibly do them all. Which ones should he do for the contest?

"Hi, Matt."

He turned around, and there was Melissa. "I came to see you whip Riley." She grinned at him, but there was a pleading look in her huge green eyes. "I'm . . . sorry I haven't had time to hang out lately."

He didn't answer. He just stood there, waiting to see if she had anything more to say. "I, um, heard you were cleared. I mean, that you didn't do any of that stuff they said you did."

"Yeah? So?" he said, keeping his distance.

"So . . . that's cool," she said. "I knew you couldn't have done that stuff, anyway. But it's cool that you didn't get in any trouble." She paused. "So . . . who do you think actually did it? Riley?"

Matt shrugged. "I don't know," he said. "Probably. But I'm not gonna go making any accusations. That's what *they* did to *me.*"

"Right," she said, biting her lip. "Well — good luck today." She leaned forward and gave him a kiss on the cheek.

A few weeks ago, that would have really made him happy. Not now. The only people who hadn't given him the cold shoulder had been Uncle Clayton and Spengler. They were okay with him. As for everyone else, well, he'd forgive them in time, but not yet. First he had to prove something — to them and to himself.

Uncle Clayton came back from parking the truck. "Whew!" he said. "What a madhouse!"

"Yeah, but there's only four of us competing in eighth grade," Matt said.

"Wow," Clay said, his eyes widening. "Okay, all the better for us. Is that kid you talked about . . . ?"

"Yeah, he's in it."

"Good. But remember, Matt — it's just you and the mountain."

"Me and the mountain."

"That's right." Clay gave him a clap on the shoulder. "Lookin' good, dude," he said. "Just apply the mind." He tapped a finger to his forehead. "I'll be sending you the vibes from the stands."

"Thanks, Uncle Clayton." Matt hugged him, and they did their usual elaborate handshake. Then Clay turned and walked off to get a good seat toward the front of the lodge's gigantic deck.

Matt went outside, fastened on his board, and slid over to the jump lift. As he rode to the top, he sat next to a girl with long, straight blond hair. She wore a hearing aid in her left ear and a contestant's number — 8/3 — on her chest. Matt's number was 8/4.

"Sally?" he asked her. "Sally Spitzer?"

She turned to him, smiled, and nodded.

"Matt Harper," he said, offering his hand.

She shook it. "You're new in school," she said, speaking a little louder than necessary, as people with hearing problems sometimes did.

"Yeah," he said. "I haven't seen you before."

But he *had* seen her. He just hadn't *noticed* her. Or rather, he'd noticed her hearing aid and tuned the rest of her out, without even realizing it.

"So, you board, huh?"

"Yeah," she said. "I'm not that good, but I love boarding more than anything. Plus, I didn't want to just let Riley Hammett win."

"You don't like Riley?"

"He's mean," she said, as if it were a big secret. "He says mean things about me all the time. He thinks I can't hear him whispering to his friends, but I can read his lips." Two big tears formed in her eyes.

"Riley's going down today," Matt promised her. He admired this girl for her courage. And he shared her passion for snowboarding. "Gimme five on it."

They slapped hands and hopped off the lift at the top of the ramp slope.

And there was Riley Hammett, waiting for them. He wore a bright yellow outfit with a sign saying 8/2 plastered to his chest and back. To his left, Matt saw Perkins wearing 8/1. They were all here. It was time to do what he'd come here to do.

The contest officials gathered them together. "We're on a tight schedule," said Mr. Evans, Matt's home-room teacher, who was serving as chief judge of the contest. "Got to get you out of here by eleven so the sixth graders can come in. So you'll each have

131

approximately one minute to prepare for each jump. You'll go at the sound of the whistle." He blew it to let them know what it sounded like.

Sally raised her hands in frustration. "I can't hear that," she said.

"Well, I'm sorry, young lady, but —"

"Listen," Matt broke in, "why don't you give a hand signal, too, so *everybody* gets it?"

Mr. Evans thought for a moment, then said, "Very well. That sounds like a good idea. I'll go like this." He brought his arm down in a comical way that made all the contestants laugh.

It was the last time any of them would laugh until the contest was over. And not all of them would be laughing then, either.

"You get one practice jump each," Mr. Evans said.

They went in order, with 8/1 going first. Perkins had obviously been practicing. He did a very nice jump with a smooth landing. Nothing fancy, but then, everyone would be saving his or her best jump for the actual contest. Riley was next. He did a spectacular grab in midjump and landed so smoothly, barely any snow was disturbed. "Just to show everyone who's boss," Matt muttered under his breath.

Then he remembered to take his mind off Riley and keep it on himself and the mountain. He missed Sally's practice jump because he was concentrating on his preparation, but he did hear the cheer that went up from the bottom of the jump, where the crowd was gathered. So. She was good. . . .

Never mind. Just me and the mountain. Matt stared down the ramp to the jump-off point, then slid into his ride. He let the jump come to him and took the air easily, relaxing into it. At the top, he felt a rush of exhilaration. He knew he'd never jumped this high before. Immediately, he pulled his concentration back onto the landing, which he made with just a little wobble.

Okay. He was ready. *Bring it on!* he thought. *Here comes Snowboard Champ.*

Now the contest began in earnest. They were to jump in the same order the first time, then shuffle the order so it would be fair to everyone.

On the first jump, Perkins fell badly. At first, Matt thought he'd been hurt, but he got up slowly and made his way back to the lift for another run.

Riley repeated his midair grab and landed perfectly, putting on the pressure. Again, Matt missed Sally's jump because he was busy getting ready for his own.

Again, he heard the cheers, which seemed even louder than those for Riley.

Matt had chosen to do a chicken salad for an appetizer, then give them the roast beef for the main entrée. For dessert, it would be a 360 and his own Combination Special. That is, he'd do it that way unless circumstances changed. If Riley should happen to, oh, say, break his leg, then . . .

Me and the mountain . . . me and the mountain . . . Again, Matt had to force himself back into focus. He made his jump, but it wasn't quite as good as his practice jump. When the scores went up after the first round, he was in third place behind Sally and Riley.

Wait a minute — *Sally was in first place?*

This time she went first, and he watched her jump — a high-flying 180 half-cab. She landed fakie and thrust her fists into the air. Even Matt found himself cheering, although he noticed that Riley wasn't.

Riley's second jump was also a half-cab. Midjump, he boned it, straightening out one leg and grabbing the board with one hand. He landed perfectly and waved to acknowledge the applause from below.

Matt stuck with his plan. His chicken salad was second nature to him now, and he needed to feel comfortable in what he was doing. Later in the contest, if he fell behind, he would pull out all the stops.

He lifted off perfectly again — the result of his constant practicing — and in midjump, he decided to add a little waggle, just for effect. The whoop of appreciation he got when he landed told him it had gone over big-time.

Sure enough, the leaderboard had bunched up. Perkins brought up the rear after his first-round fall, even though his second jump had been clean. The other three were neck and neck going into the third round.

Riley was first this time, and he brought out the big gun — the 360 turn. He wobbled a little on the landing, though, and Matt sensed an opening. For the third time, he had to remind himself to shut the other boarders out of his thoughts. He would stick with his plan and do the roast beef. There would be time for a 360 on his last jump.

He took off, started his jump, and hit the ramp edge just right. Boy, he was getting a lot of height today! Then, in midjump, he realized he'd gotten *too much* height. Thinking quickly, he tucked his head under, forcing his body into a somersault. Dizzy, staring at the snow from upside down, he navigated himself into landing position by feel alone — and hit it!

With some flailing, he managed somehow not to fall. The shouts of the onlookers rang in his ears — or maybe it was just the blood pounding, driven by his racing heart. He had improvised in midjump and landed something so spectacular not even Uncle Clayton had thought of it! A full head-over-heels somersault!

The leaderboard now showed him at the top, and by a comfortable margin. Riley was really going to have to do something amazing and stick it on the landing, too.

Sally shook her head at him in amazement. "Where have *you* been hiding?" she asked admiringly.

"It was a total accident," Matt told her truthfully.

"Yeah, right," she said with a laugh. "You're awesome!"

"Well, thanks," Matt said humbly. He knew there was still one jump to go. He still had to land it to win.

He did. His 360 was a little short, but he hit the ground with no problem. Safe at the bottom, he watched as Riley prepared for his last jump.

Even from down here, Matt could see the tension in Riley's body as he pushed off. He took off into the air and tried to do what Matt had done — a full somersault. Matt held his breath. Could Riley land the dangerous jump?

No. Riley wiped out on his landing and lay there motionless. The contest officials rushed as fast as they could through the snow toward him, but when they got there, Riley was already on his feet, pushing them away. Matt realized that Riley wasn't hurt, he was just furious. He'd been beaten in one part of the competition. The half-pipe was his only chance to save his reputation.

Sally had come in second in the jumps. "You were incredible," she told him as they walked together over to the half-pipe area.

"Thanks," he said. "I appreciate that, coming from you."

"What do you mean?" she asked, looking ready to be hurt.

"I mean, you're an awesome boarder," he said.

She brightened instantly. "Really?"

"Come on," he said. "You know you're good."

She shrugged adorably. "I guess. Anyway, good luck."

"You, too." They shook hands. "Hey," he said, hanging

137

on to her hand. "You . . . want to go boarding sometime?"

"You mean, just us?"

"Yeah, you know . . ."

"Sure!"

"Cool." He stuck his hands back into his pockets. *Yeah, Sally was all right,* he thought. So what if she wore a hearing aid? She was cool. And man, could she snowboard!

Perkins went first on the practice run. He took air a couple of times, but Matt could see he was discouraged. Matt was sorry to see it. If more kids had entered the contest, kids who maybe weren't as good as the three of them, Perkins wouldn't have looked so bad by comparison. Well, maybe next year kids wouldn't be so afraid to enter.

Matt lined up for his practice run and felt Riley's angry eyes on him. Things were great around this town until you showed up, Matt could almost hear him thinking.

Well, great for *who?* Matt was sure things would be better for most kids around here once Riley Hammett was taken down a peg or two.

He did an easy practice run just to get the feel of the

course. He had a program in mind for the various turns in the half-pipe, but he didn't want to give them away beforehand. Unlike the ramp slope, the half-pipe was icy today. Matt could feel himself slipping a little here and there. He'd have to be careful on his runs, but then again, so would everybody else.

Now the real runs began. Sally fell right near the top, but this was not fatal on the half-pipe. Since each run consisted of several airs, it was possible to regain enough speed and momentum to score a few points farther down.

Perkins fell, too. Twice. After his run, he sat on the bench near the half-pipe, head in his hands. Matt tried to catch his eye to give him a thumbs-up. Before he could, Riley sat down next to the bigger boy, threw an arm around his hunched shoulders, and started whispering in his ear. Perkins listened for a minute, then sat bolt upright and stared at Riley with what looked like disbelief. Riley shrugged, got up, and left, a nasty smile playing about his lips.

Moments later, Perkins undid his bindings and waved his arms, indicating that he was through. It didn't take a genius to realize that Riley had said something that had convinced Perkins to bow out.

Matt felt sad for him. Winning wasn't everything, he knew. Just finishing the competition was worth something, too. It showed you cared, and that you tried, and that you didn't give up. It took courage. And Perkins had been *dis*-couraged.

Matt started his first run. Ollie here, mute there, stale, method, stale, and a final 180 — and he was done. A clean first run. Enough to put more pressure on Riley. From his spot among the crowd at the bottom, he watched as Riley started down the half-pipe.

From the start, Riley was brilliant. His tricks were more distinctive, his airs higher and longer, and his speed greater than Matt's. But Matt had felt the slipperiness of the slope, and he knew Riley was playing a dangerous game. Sure enough, near the bottom, Riley wiped out, slipping out from under on a landing. He slid to the bottom and pounded on the hard snow with his fists in frustration.

Matt could sense final victory almost within his grasp. If he made a clean run on his second attempt, there was no way Riley could catch him.

Riley was approaching him now. The two of them were a little apart from the crowd and just out of earshot. "I guess you think you're the big cheese," Riley said in a low growl.

"Not really," Matt said.

"You've been lucky so far," Riley said. "But it can't last. You're not that good, Harper."

"We'll see," Matt said, willing himself to stay calm in the hopes that Riley would give up.

But Riley didn't. "Where's your mother?" Riley taunted. "She couldn't come to see you today? They wouldn't let her out on a weekend pass?"

"You don't know anything about my mother!" Matt snapped.

"Oh, yeah? She dumped you here, didn't she? Doesn't that say enough about her? About you?"

"Take that back," Matt said between clenched teeth.

"Make me," Riley said, taking a step closer.

Matt raised his fist, then slowly lowered it. "Oh, no, you don't," he said. "Say what you want now. We'll see what you say later."

He was angry now, and no matter how much he tried not to think of Riley as he prepared his run, he couldn't help it.

Riley went first this time, and Matt had to admit it was a beautiful run. Perfect. In fact, it was so good that it might put him at the top if Matt didn't do his very best.

Now he had to wait while Sally did her second run. Time to stew over Riley's comments. Time to get more and more upset.

Wait a minute! he told himself. *Stop it! Cut it out,* now!

He tried to make his heart stop beating so fast.

Me and the mountain . . . me and the mountain . . .

It wasn't working.

And then he spotted Sally. She was at the bottom of the slope, and she had her hands together, as if in prayer.

He had to do it, for her. For her and Spengler and Perkins and all the other kids Riley Hammett had made miserable all this time. Not for him — for *them.* He would do it for them, because he was . . . *Snowboard Champ!*

Snowboard Champ takes off down the half-pipe. He swerves into his first air, twirling a swift 180. Down into the pipe, then up for a full 360! Down and up, down and up — he anticipates the slip on the landings, always ready. There! One more, and one last 360, and . . . out!

The cheers were deafening. Matt knew as soon as he pulled to a stop that he'd won the contest. Uncle Clayton came plowing through the snow and gave him a bear hug. There was Spengler, raising his cast to slap him five with it. And here was Melissa, waiting to congratulate him.

Where was Sally, he wondered? Well, he would find her later and give her a gigantic high-five. Heck, maybe he'd even buy her an ice cream soda to celebrate. This was a victory for them both — and, if Matt had his way, it would soon be a victory for all the other kids Riley and his cronies had made fun of over the years.

Epilogue

Matt had lots of friends after that. Everyone wanted to be around him. In fact, it got to be a problem sometimes, like when he wanted to get some schoolwork done. He and Sally went snowboarding all the rest of that winter, and when his cast came off, Spengler joined them. It turned out that he was as good as either of them, although you wouldn't have known it to look at him.

Uncle Clayton got a big promotion at the firm. Then one day, he announced to Matt that he'd quit in order to start his own firm. "I've gotta be my own boss," Clay said. "It's just the way I'm built."

Matt's mom wrote him lots of letters, and he enjoyed bragging to the other kids about her work overseas. He hoped that when she came back, she'd come here and the three of them — she, Matt, and Uncle Clayton — could live together in Dragon Valley.

Melissa and Matt became friends again, but things were never quite right between them after what had happened. And as for Riley Hammett — well, four weeks after the contest, someone (Matt was sure it was Courtney) came forward to accuse him of setting off the fire alarm that day in January. Soon after, Matt heard that Riley's parents had found a half-used can of spray paint stuffed in the back of their son's closet. Three weeks later, they pulled him out of school and sent him to a boarding school in Utah.

Spring came, and with it the end of snowboarding season. But Matt would never forget that winter — the time when he went from being a scared kid with no real home to being a real hero, the one and only SNOWBOARD CHAMP.

The #1
Sports Series
for Kids

Read them all!

*Originally published as *Crackerjack Halfback*

All available in paperback from Little, Brown and Company

Matt Christopher®

Sports Bio Bookshelf

Lance Armstrong

Kobe Bryant

Jennifer Capriati

Julie Foudy

Jeff Gordon

Wayne Gretzky

Ken Griffey Jr.

Mia Hamm

Tony Hawk

Grant Hill

Ichiro

Derek Jeter

Randy Johnson

Michael Jordan

Mario Lemieux

Tara Lipinski

Mark McGwire

Greg Maddux

Hakeem Olajuwon

Shaquille O'Neal

Alex Rodriguez

Curt Schilling

Briana Scurry

Sammy Sosa

Venus and
Serena Williams

Tiger Woods

Steve Young